The Most Dangerous Spy

By

Sharon Edwards

Grosvenor House
Publishing Limited

This book is published by
Grosvenor House Publishing Ltd
Link House
140 The Broadway, Tolworth, Surrey, KT6 7HT.
www.grosvenorhousepublishing.co.uk

This book is a work of fiction. Any resemblance to
people or events, past or present, is purely coincidental.

A CIP record for this book
is available from the British Library

ISBN 978-1-83975-074-8
eBook ISBN 978-1-83975-075-5

To mum, and in loving memory of dad.

And with thanks to Peter Raspin, Wendy Baron,
Matthew Bayes and Elizabeth Shirra.

THE MYSTERIOUS BOX

October, 1940

Nancy Brown was not born to be a secret radio interceptor during the Second World War. In fact, the War had not even started when she was born, in 1929. It started ten years later. She remembers the day. It was a Sunday in September. She had been at church; with her family when, after the service, she noticed the grown-ups whispering to each other. Suddenly, Mother appeared in front of her; her face looking pained. She took Nancy's hand and swept her outside. Only when they were half-way home did she stoop down and whisper four words into Nancy's ear: "We are at War."

The adults talked about nothing else for weeks, but at first it made little difference to Nancy's life. She still went to school, she was still best friends with Joyce, who lived next door, and she didn't have any brothers to worry about being called up. But then, around a year after that day at church, things took a dramatic change. That was when the bombing started.

People had always said Orethorpe would be a prime target – with its four large factories – Granvilles, Langleys, Thorpe and Price and Gobley and Sons - all churning out vital contributions to the War effort. The first night it happened Nancy was at home as usual. The sudden burst of the loud electronic wailing of the air raid siren made her jump. There had been a few false alarms but she had still not got used to it and wondered if she ever would. Mother, who was sat just a few feet away, quickly wound up her knitting and placed it in a basket at her feet.

"Come on then, quickly," she said, sounding impatient. Nancy's older sister Mary had already got up from the table and had walked through the kitchen where she had opened the door onto the back yard. She stood in the yard staring into the sky. Mother grabbed three gas masks from the sideboard.

Nancy, Mary and Mother walked down the yard. As she glanced up, Nancy could see the criss-crossing of searchlights in the sky overhead. She dipped her head and saw the bulk of the air raid shelter in front of her. Father had covered the floor and part of the walls with old newspapers but the air stank of mould and the earth felt hard, cold and wet when Nancy sat down. She wrapped her old woollen cardigan tightly around her and pulled her knees up to her chest.

"Where is your father?" said Mother, sighing deeply. She pushed the makeshift door ajar so she could see him when he came.

"Do you want me to go and fetch him?" asked Nancy.

"No, no of course not, it's not safe. Oh, where is he?" said Mother.

They waited, but there was no sign of Father. Overhead Nancy could hear a whirling sound she hadn't heard before. Mother grew more impatient with each passing minute. Eventually she hauled herself up, pushed the door open and within a few seconds was striding down to the bottom of the yard, towards Dad's shed.

Ten minutes passed and there was still no sign of their parents. Suddenly Mary roused herself. "If she can disappear I can nip to the lav," she said, crawling towards the door.

"Me too, I want to go," said Nancy.

The outside toilet was only a few yards away.

"We'll have to pee in the dark as usual," said Mary, going in first. "I can't lock the door so just hold it for me."

Not long later Nancy heard the toilet flush. Mary opened the door from the inside. "Rushed it so bad I've got pee halfway down my leg," she said, giggling.

Nancy went inside. The smell was as musty and cold as that inside the shelter, but at least it was a familiar place. Afterwards she pulled the door open, but as she did so she suddenly caught sight of what seemed to be a black, rectangular box poking out at the far end of the toilet next to where Mother kept the pail and mop and other bits and pieces. It was a solid, dark mass which was scarcely visible in all the clutter. Nancy's heart began to race.

"There's a bomb in here, there's a bomb!" she shrieked.

"Oh, very funny," said Mary, holding the door open.

"It's there, it's there!" shouted Nancy again, pointing to the almost hidden object.

Mary peered around the door. At that moment Mother and Father appeared together, walking up the yard.

"Girls, what are you doing? Get back in the shelter," said Mother.

"There's a bomb," said Nancy.

"Where?" Father dashed into the toilet and stood next to Nancy. On seeing the object he immediately ran

3

over and knelt down and bent his head to put his ear next to it.

"Is it ticking?" asked Nancy.

"No, it's not," said Father.

"If a bomb had landed in our privy it'd be bigger than this and we'd have been blown to kingdom come," said Mother.

Father remained bent over the box which, on closer inspection, now appeared to be a suitcase. Reaching out, he unclipped the clasps and lifted the lid. "It's some kind of radio with wires and what look like headphones," he said. He stretched himself upright. "I don't right know what it is but it's not going to blow us up." He looked across to his wife. "What do you think my dear?"

But Mother didn't have a chance to respond because at that moment the earth beneath their feet seemed to give way. It was more than an almighty boom: it was a detonation of everything they knew, as if the very air and space that surrounded them on that cold night had been covered with gunpowder and ignited. The force sent everyone to the ground of the privy. Dust from the ceiling began to rain down on them. What followed was several seconds of silence. Someone began to cough.

"Is everyone all right? Margaret, Mary, Nancy?" her father called out from the far side. Nancy's mother and sister mumbled in reply; but, even though she tried to respond, the dust in her mouth, the ringing in her ears and the terror in her bones left Nancy unable to speak.

"Where's Nancy?" came her father's voice again. He was seated against the far wall of the privy, propped up between the sink and the black suitcase.

"She's 'ere," said Mother, reaching out her hand to touch Nancy's shoulder. Her daughter turned her face to her mother, her eyes squeezed tight and her small body trembling violently from the convulsive power of terror.

The morning after the bombing Nancy was awoken by the sound of her mother scraping out the grate of a fireplace downstairs. Sound travelled quickly through their small, terraced house, especially when Mother was busy. On opening her eyes Nancy remembered the night before and quickly pulled the blankets over her head. "How utterly embarrassing to have fainted like that," she thought to herself.

Last night, after the blast, Father had carried her back into the house. She'd been aroused by the horrid, metallic taste of liquid being poured from a bottle. Whatever it was it seemed to calm her. An hour later she was in bed, staring blankly at the red and orange colours dancing against one of the walls in the room. Real bombs had landed on Orethorpe for the first time.

On awaking the bedroom somehow seemed colder. Nancy looked across to the bed belonging to her elder sister, Audrey. It was empty. Nancy shivered, hoping Audrey, the one born between Mary and herself, had made it to a friend's house after her shift at the factory had ended. Nancy finally threw back the blankets and hauled her body into the freezing air of the bedroom. She dressed quickly, as a defence against the cold, before going downstairs. On opening the door separating the living room from the stairs she saw her mother on her knees before the fireplace.

"Now then pet? What's doing?" She looked up at Nancy with a warm smile.

"Where got bombed?" asked Nancy weakly. She'd slid into one of the easy chairs against the wall.

"Tanners Lane got hit bad. Reckon as many as five houses or more went down."

Mother eased herself up onto her feet and disappeared into the kitchen. Several minutes later she re-emerged with a plate and placed it in front of her youngest daughter. Nancy ate her breakfast in silence. Afterwards she decided to go down into the yard to see Dad in his shed.

The weak sunshine of early October had crept around the back wall of the yard and cast itself down one side. Nancy stepped from the shadows into the meagre warmth of its rays. Everything was so still, so different from last night. She opened the door to the shed and poked her head inside. As usual it was a confused mess of newspapers, wires, coils, planks of wood and tiny electric bulbs. Father lifted his head to greet her. "Nice of you to join the land of the living," he said cheerfully. When he wasn't working at the factory he spent many of his waking hours in here. Everyone called him a 'ham' and for ages Nancy hadn't known what that meant. Then she'd learned what it meant to be a ham; or, rather, a radio ham. It meant you liked building radio sets, and he did – a lot.

"Did I make a complete fool of myself last night?" asked Nancy, to which Father just laughed.

"Not at all my dear," he said, his grey eyebrows dancing up and down. "It gave us all a nasty fright. Rather a rude awakening for everyone if you ask me."

Nancy wandered further into the shed. Sometimes Father would allow her to play with the radio sets. It was one of her favourite things to do. Today, though, she wasn't drawn to the sets as she usually was. Instead, her eyes came to rest on the suitcase propped up against the back wall. Just then she heard voices in the yard. She swung around and saw Mother walking towards the shed. Behind her was a tall, thin-looking man in a heavy, blue coat. He was wearing a hat. With him was a young, red-haired boy, about Nancy's age.

"Ernie, a man is here to look at that thing we found last night," shouted Mother through the doorway.

All three entered the shed. Father stood up to welcome them. The tall man removed his hat and smiled.

"Thank you for alerting us Mr Brown; we've come to remove the article for inspection," he said.

"Yes, of course, it's just here," said Father. He reached over and picked up the suitcase. Just as he went to hand it over the tall man spoke again.

"Might I prevail upon you for a few words in private?" he asked.

"Well, yes, yes," said Father. He glanced over towards his wife.

"Come up to the kitchen to help me out," said Mother to Nancy.

The pair walked up to the house. Once inside the kitchen Nancy turned to face the yard. The shed door had been closed. Ten minutes later the sound of voices could be heard again, coming towards the house. Father and the man and boy walked through the kitchen and into the living room. Mother stood up to greet them once more but Father quickly ushered them into the front room before he opened the door into the street. There were more muffled voices and then the sound of the door closing.

7

"Everything all right, dear?" asked Mother. Father appeared from the front room.

"Yes, my dear; now I've some work to catch up on so I'll be in the shed," he said, walking towards the kitchen door. A few moments later Nancy watched him disappear down the yard.

GUIDE NIGHT

1940

A few days after the bombing Nancy and Father walked through the streets of Orethorpe, she in her Guide uniform and he carrying an old leather satchel which was so full that it bulged out at every angle. They picked their way along the pavement in the dark. Every Tuesday evening her local Guide group would gather inside the cold church rooms to do whatever energetic activities the leaders could think of to keep them warm and aid the War effort.

Normally, Father would see her through the front door before he would turn to leave, but tonight he had promised Nancy that he would help her set up the equipment for her telegraphist badge. The pair walked into the room and made their way over to a table in the corner. Father opened the satchel and began to empty the contents onto the table. There was a main box with its dials and holes, a set of headphones and a Morse key. It was all that was needed for a basic wireless receiver, and had been carefully put together by Nancy and Father in his shed.

"Let's have a run-through, eh lass?" said Father, his enthusiasm for anything to do with radio showing through. "You plug the headphones in here you see, and the Morse key."

"Dad, you're not supposed to show me," Nancy whispered, her eyes wandering over to Miss Jolly, the Guide Captain, to make sure she wasn't listening. "I'll be okay; you go back home."

"Okay lass, if you're sure," he said. He began to walk towards the door, but then stopped. Looking across the room, Nancy saw him talking to a man. He wore a long, dark overcoat and had a hat. Nancy had seen the hat before. It belonged to the man who had collected the mysterious case from the house. Beside him was a boy around her age, the same one who had also come to the house the day after the bombing.

"What are *they* doing here?" she wondered.

"...a very special guest." Nancy's attention swung back to Miss Jolly, who was standing in the middle of the room shouting out instructions as she went over to the man and shook hands. She was galloping out her words and making exaggerated hand gestures across the room.

Nancy turned back towards her table. "Will they give us the same message as last week?" The question came from Fiona who was standing close to Nancy. She was also taking her telegraphist badge that night.

"Shouldn't think so: what would be the point?" replied Nancy. "It wouldn't be a real test then, would it?"

After a few minutes she heard Miss Jolly's voice again. "These are the pair doing their child nurse badges tonight," she said. Miss Jolly and the man and boy had moved over to her side of the room. Two other Guides, Hester and Tilly, were bent over a small, tin bath. Each held a toy baby over the bath and pretended to wash it with their free hands. The man looked on with a smile.

"Thank you girls," said Miss Jolly after a few minutes. She was using the brisk tone of voice she used when other adults were in the room. "And here," she said, turning to Nancy and Fiona, "here we have something that will interest you. These girls are taking their telegraphist badge tonight." The group took a couple of steps towards her table. Miss Jolly continued: "Now then girls, this gentleman is overseeing the War effort on the Home Front, and I've been telling him all about your talent for Morse code, Nancy." She turned back to the man and the boy. "Oh yes," she said, "Nancy has something of a talent for Morse code and can build a radio receiver in a trice, not that that should be a surprise to any of us. Her Father is a big radio enthusiast, isn't he Nancy?"

Nancy's bottom lip quivered. Normally she would have talked with gusto about her father's love of radio, but her mind suddenly jumped back to that strange case and the man's visit to her Father. She glanced up to meet the man's eyes. "Yes," she said firmly, before she looked down again.

"We're delighted to hear it: and what does a Guide have to do?" he asked. She glanced up again and saw him smiling at her. He was rather distinguished looking and carried an air of authority about him.

"Build a wireless receiver," said Nancy, her voice firm.

"And what else, Nancy?" asked Miss Jolly.

"Send a Morse code message at thirty words a minute."

"And do you know what Morse code is?" he asked.

"Yes, of course: it's a system of turning letters into sounds that can be made by hitting a key on a hard surface. My father has told me all about it."

11

He clapped his hands loudly. "Excellent," he said. "They use it to fool us and we use it to fool them, eh? And will you give us a demonstration?"

Nancy leant over the black box receiver. It was small and looked like a radio set, with its dials and coils. She plugged the headphones into the socket and took out a small pebble-looking object from the table.

"What's that?" asked Miss Jolly.

"It's the crystal that finds the right frequency," said Nancy.

The crystal had its own slot and she plugged that in too. Then the Morse key was attached. Finally she poised the index finger of her right hand over the Morse key and began to tap out a message. After a few minutes she stopped tapping and looked up.

"Morse is a language system used for sending messages over radio waves," she said. "You connect the Morse key to the machine and it connects with a radio wave so the Morse can be sent over the airwaves to be heard by other people."

"Wonderful work, simply wonderful, that's the way to show em, eh?" said the man. Nancy looked up and saw his eyes fixed on her.

"And why do we need Morse?" he asked Nancy.

"The Army and other military use it," she replied. "It's a way of getting messages to each other very quickly."

"And a lot more besides," he said. He was staring at her again, making Nancy feel uneasy. The man and boy hovered for a few minutes more before they moved on to other tables to view Brenda's knitting, hear Judith's ideas on raising money to buy blankets for people in the bombed-out areas, and advise Andrea on the best tracking techniques. But every now and again Nancy would see the man glance back towards her and the box of dials and wires at her side.

THE DROP

1940

The following Saturday meant a walk to the shops with Mother. They set off through the narrow streets, which eventually opened up into the wide square of the market area with the shops. After the queues and the shopping they would head to Brents, Orethorpe's only department store. Its Rose Garden café served hot tea in delicate china cups. Nancy and Mother would sit in the café, with their gas masks on their laps and their shopping bags crammed under the table, and savour every sip while their eyes wandered around the semi-luxurious surroundings so different from home.

This Saturday Nancy and Mother sat in virtual silence and, when it came time to return home, Nancy watched her mother lean down to scoop up the shopping bags with a deep sigh. They made their way down the back stairs of the store and onto Monks Street. But as she stepped into the fresh air Nancy didn't see the usual bustle of the town, but a scene of hurry and bluster against the sudden whining noise of the sirens.

"Everyone into the air raid shelter!" shouted a man in a grey coat. He had a piece of cloth wrapped around his arm, but Nancy couldn't make out the letters printed on it.

"What now, it's daylight!" exclaimed Mother. For the first time since the start of the War, Nancy heard a catch of fear in her voice.

The man glanced over at them. "Follow the line of people down to the right; the underground shelter is open. Don't dawdle there, please; keep everyone moving, down there, down there," he pointed again, with greater urgency this time.

A few seconds later she and Mother were being swept along by the ribbon of people streaming from the shops and cafés, boys in short trousers, men in caps, rich-looking women in fur shawls and the not-so-rich in old tweed coats. They reached the top of the huge stone steps that led down to the public shelter. A queue had formed at the top and a man and a woman wearing the same arm-bands as the man on the street were filtering the crowd down, into the darkness.

"What's goin' on, is Hitler bombing us during the day as well as the night?" shouted a man in front of them. A few people glanced around and muttered to each other or themselves. The man and woman ignored him and continued giving instructions of their own.

"Careful on the stairs. Madam, can you help this good lady? Thank you, see she gets to sit down." Nancy saw a man take the arm of a very old lady. She watched their heads bob down the stairs until they disappeared. She and Mother edged close to the top of the stairs. "Just be patient a little longer and everyone will get inside in good time. There's about thirty steps. Is it what? Yes, it's lit. Someone at the bottom will show you where to go."

Ten minutes later Nancy was shuffling along a narrow, underground corridor amongst a sea of bodies, coats, bags and staring faces.

"Move down, move down, don't crowd at the front," someone behind her was shouting.

Nancy picked her way along the corridor, aware of Mother behind her. Wooden benches lined the walls on both sides, leaving just enough room to walk down the centre. Nancy could now see a line of people sitting on the benches stretching out in front of her. She could go no further. Seeing a spare patch of bench she quickly sat down. Mother managed to get a seat beside her. The tunnel was filling up and as she glanced down towards the entrance Nancy thought she saw the ginger hair and face of someone familiar bobbing in and out of the crowd. She saw it briefly before it disappeared behind a large man. Then it appeared again. It suddenly dawned on her who it was. It was the boy who came to the house that day and the Guide meeting as well. A few moments later he dodged around a couple and their two children and began striding towards them. He sat down on the bench opposite.

"This is quite a do, isn't it?" he said.

Mother looked at him curiously.

"Mother, this is…" Nancy suddenly realised she didn't even know his name.

"It's Tom," he said, grinning.

"How do you do, Tom," said Mother, in the polite tone she used for strangers.

"Hello," he replied, grinning again.

"And where do you live, Tom?"

Nancy realised that Mother hadn't recognised Tom from his visit to the house to collect the mysterious case.

"In Halfpen' Street," he said. He'd removed his cap and was twisting it around in his hands.

"Halfpenny Street," said Mother, partly to confirm that she'd heard him and partly to correct his pronunciation.

For the next two hours Nancy sat squashed between Mother on one side and a stranger on the other. It grew hot and sticky and she felt herself getting drowsy. Occasionally, Nancy would glance at Tom and he would catch her eye and give her the strangest, knowing look. Neither the sound of sirens nor bombing could be heard, so it was to huge groans of relief that the all-clear eventually came. They were funnelled out of the tunnel the same way they came in, and as she climbed the stone steps Nancy could feel the sharp air of the outdoors on her face. Nancy and Mother quickly walked away from those streaming out from the top of the stairs. Nancy noticed that Tom was close behind them.

After a minute or so Mother swung around to face Nancy. "I've left my hat in the shelter," she said.

"I'll get it," said Tom. He reached out for Nancy's hand, "We'll go together and catch you up." With that he pulled Nancy away and soon they were hurrying along. "Don't say anything, just come with me," he whispered with great urgency.

"Where are we going?" Nancy cried. She tried to yank her hand away but he was pulling at her again.

"Come on, do you want to win this War or don't you?" he said in a low whisper.

They walked quickly into the street that ran parallel with the Market Square. Dusk was coming on the town fast and Nancy knew that they would soon struggle to see. But still Tom strode on, past the terraced houses and out towards the fields. They came to a gate.

"What are you doing?" asked Nancy. "If we go in there we'll never find our way out."

Tom turned towards her. "Oh yes we will, it's a full moon tonight and they always use that."

"They? Who's they?"

But Tom had bolted over the gate and was already striding ahead. Nancy hovered at the gate for a few moments before she, too, climbed over and began to follow him. They took hurried steps across the fields for several minutes until Tom suddenly raised his hand.

"See that?" he said, pointing ahead. And she *could* see it, a small white light in the line of trees on the other side of the field ahead. First it was there, then it disappeared, then appeared again.

"They'll be here soon," whispered Tom. "Look, we can watch from over there." He pointed to a large, stone feeding trough jutting out of the ground. They ran to it and crouched down. Each peered around the trough on different sides, looking towards the trees.

"Who is it?" whispered Nancy.

"You'll soon see," he whispered back.

The white light grew stronger now. Straining to see in the dark, Nancy realised she could make out the figure of someone emerging from the woodland. Whoever it was had the light in one hand, for it bobbed up and down. Then she saw a second figure walk over to the first. The two ghost-like figures stood together. She went to speak but was stopped suddenly by a sound overhead. Quickly Nancy could make out the unmistakable sound of aircraft.

"It's the Germans, the Luftwaffe; we've got to get out of here." Her whisper had taken on an urgent, desperate tone. But Tom didn't move his gaze from the two figures.

"It's not a bombing raid," he said knowingly.

The overhead engine was getting closer until suddenly Nancy could see a plane's brooding, black bulk in the sky. She was starting to panic, believing they'd never survive a bomb at this close range. A sudden impulse to run overwhelmed her and, without thinking, she uncurled her body and stood up, ready to flee. But it was then that she saw three graceful parachutes wafting through the night air, towards the ground. Attached to each of them was the outline of a body. The two figures also watched, and when the three bodies had landed they ran over to each in turn. Nancy and Tom watched as the parachutes were thrown over each stranger's shoulder and all the figures disappeared again into the woods. By then the aircraft sound was distant again. It hadn't even landed.

"Wow!," Tom whistled between his teeth. "Did you see that? What a whizz seeing that."

BANG BANG BANG! Suddenly she heard the crack of gunfire across the field. Nancy ducked her head back and scrunched her body low towards the ground.

"Help, help!" she began to scream, but her voice was drowned out in the shrill whistling and then the frantic shouting in front of her. There was more gunfire, more shouting. She bolted upright, turned back towards the way they had come and began to run harder and faster than she had ever attempted in her life. After a few moments she became aware of Tom running behind her. They ran and ran, over the fields, scrambling over gates and sloshing through streams until, at last, they came to the edge of the town.

It wasn't until they reached Coleridge's store on the corner of Sheepwash Street that they dared stop to lean their shaking legs against the boarded-up windows and take huge gulps of breath. Eventually Nancy spoke. "Who are they Tom? Who are they?" Tom's face was red, his breath panting and his hair matted with sweat. "Who are they?" She was almost shouting now.

"Haven't you guessed yet? They're German spies of course." He stared into her astonished face. "They're spies!"

MR SMITH

June 2010

At the end of a long driveway on the outskirts of Orethorpe was a large house in the grip of a slow decay. The outside brickwork was coarse and a faded muddy colour. The windows were streaked with bird mess, their wooden frames dry and cracked like the skin on a very old man or woman. Only a few ancient brushstrokes of paint had managed to cling to the woodwork. It was a rusty colour, as if it had once been a bright red, like an aunt's lipstick when she bent down to kiss an unwilling niece or nephew.

Inside the large, faded kitchen Mr Smith laid the table for tea. He was an old man who shuffled around slowly. His clothes hung on his thin frame, but his eyes were bright, especially today, for he was preparing for a visitor. Arthur was coming; Arthur the twelve-year-old who lived close by, the boy Scout, who came once a week to tidy up his garden.

The pair had met in Orethorpe several months before, not long after Mr Smith's wife, Marion, had died. Mr Smith was on his way to the post office on his mobility scooter when he saw the figure of a lad out of the corner of his eye. Before he knew it the boy had stepped out in front of him, forcing him to slam on the brakes.

"Watch out!" he had shouted.

Arthur had sprung back and for a couple of seconds the two just stared at each other. Mr Smith, who was usually such a mild-mannered chap, was himself taken aback.

"Sorry," said Arthur faintly, before his mother appeared.

Two weeks later the Scout leader, Peter Pickles, arrived on Mr Smith's doorstep with none other than Arthur, the same boy, in tow.

"Ahem, Mr Smith, sir?" asked Mr Pickles. The old man had squinted at the two figures on his front step: one a tidy, fussy-looking man in a crisp uniform; behind him a short lad. "I'm one of the leaders of the Scouts, sir, at your service," continued the Scout Master.

"Are you? Oh, oh how, how, how, how nice," said Mr Smith.

There was another pause before Mr Pickles cleared his throat and continued. "You should have had a visit from the town council," he said. "I believe they've been round to talk about the community scheme, litter-picking, visiting, ahem, visiting older people in the nursing home, you know the kind of thing I mean. Well, ahem, we were told you'd like some help with your garden. Arthur here has volunteered to help someone with the garden once a week, cutting the grass and things. Arthur will get his Community Service Badge and, who knows, the whole pack might get a council award, eh Arthur?"

Mr Smith looked down at the boy standing beside the Scout leader. Finally he spoke. "Oh I, I, I, see," he said, looking back up to Mr Pickles. His weak voice betrayed his age. "Do you want to come inside? H-h-h-h-h hold on a second, I was just about to empty the pot." And with that he leant forward and jerked the teapot in his hand, sending its thick, brown liquid onto the ground, followed by two sodden teabags, which landed on the lawn with a squishing sound. Mr Pickles jumped sideways slightly to avoid getting splashed. He laughed nervously before the old man stepped away to allow the pair to enter, closed the door behind them and shuffled ahead and into the living room.

The room was cold and had the smell and atmosphere of damp. Mr Smith slowly levered himself into an armchair which sagged in the middle, sending a puff of dust into the air. Mr Pickles moved a jumper from a cushion so he could sit down on the edge of the sofa, ready to spring up again at any moment. He motioned for Arthur to do the same.

"Well," said Mr Pickles in a loud, over-cheerful voice, for he was feeling a little uncomfortable, both at his surroundings and at the boy's continued silence. "Arthur will call around Saturday morning around eleven and we'll see how it goes. He'll have to be accompanied by one of the other leaders for the first few weeks, health and safety and all that, you understand. But if you can let us know what kind of things he'd be required to do in the garden then I will fill in this form." He reached into his shirt pocket and pulled out a piece of paper which he hastily unfolded. "We can do most of the formalities today so they are out of the way."

"It's very, very kind of you and all the young people," said Mr Smith in his low voice. "I do manage to cut the grass now and again, you know, but it's a little hard on my old back. But it's so very obliging of you to offer to help. A-a-a-a-a are you sure it's not too much trouble?"

"No, no, that's what the Scouts are here for."

Arthur only half-listened as the two men talked. Their chatter faded into the background as he fixed his gaze on the old man. He looked with wonder at his hollow cheeks, the dark, bushy eyebrows and silver hair. The face was long and lined, his clothes faded and baggy. His eyes appeared sunken into their sockets and his Adam's apple bobbed up and down every time he spoke. Mr Smith sat with his hands clasped in front of him, and when he did speak his voice sounded nervous, like that of a boy or girl called to read aloud in front of the entire assembly at school. Occasionally, during the conversation, the old man would glance at Arthur, but the lad sat like stone on the sofa. Eventually Mr Pickles cleared his throat again and stood up.

"I've written it all down, so if you just sign here saying you're happy to have the work done," he said, passing the completed form to the old man, who squinted hard before reaching into his shirt pocket for a pen. Arthur noticed how his hand shook slightly as it hovered over the form for a moment. Then, at last, it was time to go. They walked back towards the front door, their shoes sounding hollow on the threadbare carpet. Arthur glanced at a staircase near the door. A crack had run up the wall like a ladder in a pair of his mum's tights. Mr Pickles swung round to say goodbye, holding out his hand to the old man, who took it feebly.

"Say goodbye, Arthur," said Mr Pickles suddenly, looking down at Arthur. Arthur reached out his sweaty hand to Mr Smith. The old man didn't react.

"Goodbye," said the boy, his voice betraying his nerves, as he quickly withdrew his hand. With that they left. As he and the leader walked down the path Arthur glanced back towards the house. Mr Smith was standing in the frame of the front door. He seemed to be staring into space.

The following Saturday Arthur, together with several other boys, was back at Mr Smith's house. They were accompanied by Jack Williams, another volunteer leader. The boys got to work cutting the grass, taking it in turns to push the ancient mower that they had to force through the thick carpet of lawn. It took so long that there was no time left in the hour to do anything else.

"Now the grass has been cut it won't be as hard next time," said Jack.

Arthur was relieved it was over. But the following week he was back. By the third week he was allowed to go on his own. To his young eyes the garden was the same chaotic mess as the house itself. The lawn had been allowed to grow unchecked for so long that it had spread into the soil borders. The grass itself was thick with moss and dandelions and the barely distinguishable borders were full of weeds.

By week four Arthur knew how many times he had to criss-cross the lawn with the mower and how long it would take. He kept a mental note of the number of aircraft that flew overhead and he counted how many weeds he pulled out each time. In his own little way he tried to make the time pass as quickly as he could. He would try to run with the lawn mower instead of walking. He would time how long it took him to pull out one weed every five centimetres along the borders – each time trying to do it quicker than before. He stopped raking the patch of soil furthest away from the front window, believing Mr Smith would not notice. The old man would stand at the front door each week, straining his eyes to see into the garden. Afterwards he would politely thank the boy in his weak voice, his shoulders hunched, his right hand on the wall to steady his slightly trembling frame.

THE NOTE

1940

The note was pushed into Nancy's hand as she walked home from school. She and her friend Joyce had reached Granvilles factory during the afternoon shift change. They were struggling through the crowds of men and women streaming from the gates when Nancy suddenly became aware that something had been shoved into her hand. She looked down. It was a small, brown envelope marked *Miss N Brown – Secret*. She quickly looked up but could only see hurried expressions on the faces of the weary, dirty labourers. Without thinking she shoved the envelope into her coat so that Joyce could not see. On reaching home Nancy sprinted up the narrow stairs to her bedroom. She closed the door and lifted the envelope to her eyes. She ripped it open. It read:

TOP SECRET

MINISTRY OF LABOUR & NATIONAL SERVICE

Orethorpe
Monday, 14 October, 1940

Dear Madam

I have to inform you that under Defence Regulation 29 BA you may be directed to part-time service in the police or civil defence. In this connection you are required to attend a preliminary interview at Dorehill's grocery shop, Cowpuddle Lane, Orethorpe on Saturday, 19 October, 1940, at 4.30pm.

There was no name, no signature, nothing else to say what lay ahead. She did not know what it all meant. It had only been a couple of days since she and Tom had sprinted over the fields and watched the mysterious figures with their parachutes wafting through the air, closely followed by the sound of gunfire. She had not told Mother or Father what had happened. Before she had hurried home, Tom had told her that she could never tell them because it would get him into terrible trouble with those in authority. She had hastily agreed, and something told her that they wouldn't believe her anyway. Reaching home she had mumbled something to Mother about them getting delayed, but said nothing else. Mother was so overwhelmed with relief to see Nancy safe that she let it go.

Suddenly Nancy heard a door slam downstairs, followed by mumbled voices. The catch at the door to the staircase was lifted and an unmistakable voice was heard. "I'll ask her to give me some kip." Audrey! What was she doing home? Nancy could hear her skipping up the stairs. She would be in the room in seconds. Nancy frantically opened the door to the small bedside cabinet separating the two beds and shoved the note inside. She slammed it shut. At that moment Audrey opened the door.

"What you up to then little sis, hiding a secret?" said Audrey, walking across to the dressing table and throwing herself down on the chair. She began unpinning her hair in the mirror. Audrey was prettier than Mary but with a sharper tongue. Like Father, Audrey worked at Langleys factory in town.

"Nothing, just homework, that's all," said Nancy.

"Homework? Funny isn't it, here's me and Father and thousands of others working all the hours God sends to win the War and life goes on for everyone else."

"Everyone is doing their bit," said Nancy.

"Hmm, with the Guides I suppose? Do you mind scooting off for a couple of hours so I can get some shut-eye?" Audrey smiled across at her, but it was a cold smile.

"Be my guest; I'm going to help Mother," said Nancy, striding out of the room.

THE SHOP

1940

The shop was relatively new, but looked old. It was tatty and grey-looking. A few tins had been arranged in the window. Nancy pushed the door open and walked into the cramped space. Two women stood by the counter. They were holding up plain-looking tins. One of the women held one up to her nose and was squinting her eyes. The other woman was chattering quickly. She was complaining about her lodgers.

"I never said they could use the living room when we're out and now one of them is complaining to anyone who will listen. But you know what it's like in this town, you're chewing an apple at one end of the street and it's a great big melon at the other."

"A fine thing it would be to chew on a melon," said the other woman with a deep sigh.

Nancy made her way to the large counter on one side of the room. A neat young man stood behind it.

"Can I help you, Miss?" He looked at her blankly.

"I have a, er, I mean I've come to err, well, you see, I have this." She reached into her coat pocket and pulled out the note before handing it to him. He picked it up. Then, without bothering to open it, he turned around and walked through a door behind him. Nancy expected him back any moment but she waited and waited. The room had become quiet and she looked across to where the women were standing. They had been staring at her but quickly looked away when she glanced across. After several more minutes the door to the back of the shop opened again and the man came through. He immediately walked around the counter and up to where Nancy was.

"Yes, we have that, Miss, it was handed in," he said. He held up the corner of the counter, which swung up on its hinges, and beckoned Nancy through. "If you just want to come round the back while I find it." As he was speaking he glanced over to the two women. Nancy followed him behind the counter and through the door. He quickly closed it behind her. "Good to get out of public view," he said briskly. "They all get very tetchy if they think someone's getting extra food or something. Now, if you follow me."

He led her along a narrow passageway. Wooden crates and tins were stacked up against one wall, narrowing the space even more. They came to a staircase. At the top of the stairs they turned a sharp corner and came onto a small landing. The shop assistant knocked on the first door at the top.

Nancy could hear muted voices and a moment later the door was swung open from the inside. A man had opened it. It was the same tall, thin man who had turned up at Guides that night and another, older and fatter man she didn't recognise. There was also someone else in the room. It was Tom.

The older man was the first to speak. "Come in," he said. "Miss Brown, isn't it? Yes of course it is, glad you

31

could make it." He turned away and back into the room. Nancy followed.

He beckoned her to sit on a hard chair behind a desk placed in the middle of the room. He sat down in the chair opposite. "It's good of you to come, Miss Brown," he continued. She noticed he was wearing some kind of uniform she didn't recognise.

"What do you want with me?" she asked, sitting down.

"That's right, cut to the chase, we don't mind, in fact we prefer it. Quite lucky finding you I'd say. What I mean is your radio work and the like."

"What, the Guides stuff, is that what you mean?" she replied.

"That's exactly what I mean."

"We're doing badges to help the War effort, that's all." She suddenly felt her mouth go dry and her heart pound slightly faster.

"Ha," he said, slamming his heavy hand on the desk. "And you know Morse?"

"I'm getting better at it, why?"

"How fast?" he blurted out, leaning forward over the desk towards her now.

"Up to twenty five words a minute but I'm..."

Before she had the chance to finish he slammed his hand on the desk again. "Superb, superb," he said, turning around to the tall, thin man who stood against one of the walls facing her. He also wore a uniform. The older man turned back to her. "And your German: you speak that do you?"

"We're learning at school and my teacher says I have a special skill for it."

Nancy was staring at one man and then the other. What did they want with her and how did he know about her German lessons? It was then that the tall, thin man spoke for the first time.

"The country is at War, Miss Brown; you know that, of course," he said, his tone gentle. "What you may not know is that England could be invaded by Hitler's forces." He suddenly walked over towards her, reached out to a spare chair in the corner of the room and slammed it down on the floor close to hers. He sat down and leant forward. "Hitler is coming, that's a fact, but we want to stop him," he said. "It's our duty to stop him. It's *my* duty and it's *your* duty to do whatever we can to aid our own side in keeping the Germans at bay, and *you* can help us. Do you understand?"

"We want you to listen," the older man explained, taking over from his colleague. "You know how to listen and goodness knows there aren't enough of you. Nothing to do with running into a line of bullets or trying to get yourself blown up. It's absurdly simple. We just want you to listen."

Nancy looked at the faces bearing down on her. After a few moments she blurted out: "Listen to what?"

The older man leant in even closer, their faces almost touching. "Why, the Germans, of course, German spies."

He drew his face away. "We know they're here. Why are they here? They're here because of what we, this town, are doing for the War effort. I don't know if you've noticed but the factories are busier and bigger than ever. They're churning out aeroplanes, bombs and munitions. If the spies can disturb or destroy that then they have a chance to put the entire nation's efforts back and that would make us, well, less able to resist an invasion. And I think you already know a little of what's going on from your adventure the other night."

He turned to Tom. "Do you have it?" he said. Something Nancy recognised was lifted up onto the desk with a thump. It was the strange suitcase she'd found in the family toilet on the night of the bombing. "Do you want to open it?" she was asked. She reached out and released the clasps. The top of the suitcase swung back revealing a solid black mass inside. The suitcase had been filled with a large, black box with dials and wires. Nancy saw a set of headphones had been tucked in along one side.

"This," said the older man, "is one of their communications sets. They use them to send messages to Germany and to listen to them back. *That's* what you found the other day. We have to find them, but in order to do that we have to track them, and to do that we have to listen to them. It's our best way of picking them out of a crowd of thousands of factory workers and the like that's growing in number every day. We know they have to talk to each other and the people they take orders from in Germany. But there aren't enough of us to do it. Will you listen? Will you help us find them? Will you?"

Nancy glanced around her. The room had gone silent. "I will do what I can," she said eventually, barely knowing what she was really saying.

A smile cracked across the older man's face, reaching his eyes. "I had a feeling we could trust you," he said. He reached out his hand. "Wait for instructions on what to do next, and for victory's sake tell no-one of this, you understand? Absolute secrecy is of the essence, in fact, it's more than that. Lives, people's lives, depend upon it. You'll be trained of course, up at the big house on the hill. Wait until you're called. It's called Megg House, remember that: Megg House."

MEGG HOUSE

1940

The morning of her first visit to Megg House was crisp and sunny. Nancy left the house half an hour earlier than usual. During morning registration at school a few days earlier the headteacher had read aloud a letter from the Guide movement saying she was being released for special training. "If only you knew," she'd thought.

She had been summoned, as the men in the shop had told her she would be. It happened several days after the meeting in the shop. She had been walking past the factory again after school when another note had been shoved into her hand. Again, she had been unable to tell who had put it there in the throng of people swelling out of the gates.

She only had a vague idea where Megg House was. Her instructions told her it was halfway up Manor Road, but she was certain she had never seen it there. It was only when she had climbed the steep corner that she saw the sign at the bottom of what looked like an even steeper drive through some woods. She began to climb, and on rounding another corner she saw another drive sweeping to the left before coming back again in front of a large house. To Nancy it looked like a grand vicarage or one of the expensive hotels she had seen on one of the family's rare summer trips to the seaside, one with lawns sweeping down to the beach.

She walked along the drive. Nearing one of the huge windows she stopped and looked inside. There were long benches with bare wooden seats. The room was full of men and women hunched over what looked like hundreds of pieces of paper. The men and women held pencils and occasionally she would see them make markings on the papers. Then she noticed the other main activity in the room, more men and women sat in front of big, black boxes. The people on that side of the room wore headphones. She saw a man screw up a piece of paper into a ball before throwing it at one of the women sat behind one of the boxes on the other side of the room. Unable to hear because of the noise in her headphones, the woman didn't notice until the missile landed on her head. The whole room erupted into laughter, and the door swung open and a middle-aged woman with a trolley holding cups and saucers entered.

Nancy walked on. She came to the front door and noticed it was open. Outside it was a young woman in a dark-blue uniform. She had a full face and very dark hair down to her shoulders. Her blouse was crisp white and her tie was perfect. She wore flat, polished shoes. Her fingernails were bare of polish but she made up for it by the scarlet red on her lips. She held a clipboard.

"You must be Miss Brown, yes?" she said, smiling down at Nancy.

"Yes, that's right."

"Don't look so frightened love, we don't bite. You're on time, that's a good sign. I'm Miss Halsall, one of the staff here."

She held out her hand for Nancy to take. Nancy gave a weak handshake. Miss Halsall turned into the house and waved her hand for Nancy to follow. The hallway was wide with a large staircase and several doors, all of them shut.

"Come with me please," said Miss Halsall.

Nancy was led up a slightly narrow, rather winding staircase to the first floor. They went down a corridor where, at the end, a door was open. Entering the room she saw a plain table and some matching chairs. Notepads and pencils had been placed on the table, together with three large, brown envelopes. The furniture had been arranged to face a blackboard mounted on one of the walls. To the left of the room, towards the window, Nancy noticed another table. On it were several black radios together with curly wires, three sets of headphones and what she recognised as Morse keys.

She was instructed to sit at the table. Nancy noticed that one of the large, brown envelopes was addressed to her.

"Only open it when instructed," said Miss Halsall. "Shortly, we'll begin."

After several minutes a piece of paper was placed in front of her. At the top in bold letters were the words **OFFICIAL SECRETS ACT.**

"You have to sign this or we go no further," said Miss Halsall.

Nancy signed her name at the bottom.

"This means that you tell absolutely no-one, and I mean no-one, about what you learn or see or hear at Megg House, is that understood?" said Miss Halsall. Nancy nodded. "Absolute secrecy is our single most powerful weapon, as it is for the enemy," she continued. "In order to help you with that you need to read this and remember it."

She handed Nancy another piece of paper marked SECRECY. Below it was a list of instructions.

DO NOT TALK AT MEALS: Waitresses may not be what you think.

DO NOT TALK WHILE ON PUBLIC TRANSPORT: You don't know who is listening.

DO NOT TALK BY YOUR FIRESIDE. You do more to protect your loved ones by your secrecy than anything else. After all, your work is for them.

"These are to avoid any slip-ups," said Miss Halsall. "As I said, you always need to remember the need for secrecy."

Next Nancy was instructed to open the brown envelope addressed to her. She pulled out sheets of paper stamped TOP SECRET in black print. Underneath were typed lines that Nancy struggled to understand. The first one read:

Agents in place. Awaiting further instructions.

Nancy read on.

First order to be delivered Friday. Heavy munitions. Making contacts to learn more.

She looked up. Miss Halsall was giving a knowing smile.

"Do you know what they are?" asked Miss Halsall.

"Are they secret messages?" replied Nancy.

"Correct," said Miss Halsall. "They are transmissions sent by the enemy out there." She pointed outside the window.

"Where out there?" asked Nancy.

"In the town, that's where. You are here, we are here, to find the spies working out there. They are there, I can assure you, and they're a lot closer than you think. You're here to be an interceptor, listening in to the enemy out there. I was told you already knew Morse and also how to handle a wireless."

"Well I do, but that doesn't mean…"

Miss Halsall cut in before she could finish. "In this War, here in this town, it means exactly what we say it does," she said. "We need people like you to listen in to what they're doing and what they're saying. Like I said, you're a listener, an interceptor."

Miss Halsall stood up and turned towards the blackboard against the wall. She began drawing the outline of houses, shops, streets, churches and factories. Soon Nancy recognised the outline of Orethorpe.

"This," said Miss Halsall, pointing the end of her chalk towards the centre of the town, "is where they are operating. The German spy network we know to be here."

"How many are there?" asked Nancy.

"That's top secret and that means even I don't know," said Miss Halsall. "The point is they are here and we know they're here. We're assuming it's too dangerous for them to live together or even see each other all the time so they have to communicate with each other and, most crucially, with their superiors in Germany. And we need to know what they're saying and when they're saying it. And then we might just be in with a chance of catching them. The factories are the obvious targets so we must assume that intelligence and sabotage are their main aims. They're here to find out what we're making – and then destroy it." She pointed again. "Keep this in mind when you're here. *This* is what we're protecting."

Miss Halsall threw the chalk down on a table and sat down at the table in front of her. She pulled a Morse key towards her.

"In front of you are pencils and sheets of lined paper," she said. "On my mark begin to take down and transcribe the Morse code message I am about to tap out."

Nancy only just had enough time to pick up her pencil and poise her hands over the paper when Miss Halsall's right index finger began to do its work on the key. A weak tap could be heard with every firm press of the small metal rod down onto its metal base. Tap tap, tap tap tap, tap, pause, tap tap tap. Some were close together, others spaced out, at once quick and then slower. Nancy recognised the audible dits and pauses as the mysterious language of Morse code. At first she had little trouble recognising the letters and then the words, but then the taps suddenly got faster. Nancy leant forward in an attempt to hear better, but the rapid stream of sounds had become a continuous tone. She stopped writing but Miss Halsall did not appear to notice and continued tapping out the sounds. After a while she suddenly stopped and looked up.

"Quite a struggle, eh?" said Miss Halsall. "That, if you hadn't gathered, was Morse at speed – the kind of speed you will be expected to transcribe as part of your work here."

"That's stupid," blurted out Nancy. "No-one sends that fast."

"Wrong!" said Miss Halsall sharply. "What do you think an enemy agent's number-one priority is?"

"You told me, to spy things out and destroy them and tell Germany about it," Nancy answered.

"Wrong," said Miss Halsall a second time. She leant forward. "A spy's first and foremost priority is not to get caught," she said. "They must remain hidden and undetectable. And when are they detectable? When they're on air of course. Then we can hear them and then we have a chance of tracking their signal and finding them. You know what they say, 'The enemy is listening'? Well we are their enemy and we are listening. What's more, they know it. That is why the messages to Germany must be sent as quickly as possible. Every moment on air is a moment when we, their enemy, have a chance of detecting them. For them, every extra moment is an added risk. They must send their message and send it fast before they get off air and move location – quickly. That is why you must recognise Morse at that speed – recognise it for what it is and let us know. And if you think that was hard, try taking it down in German Morse, yes, that's right, German Morse. You didn't expect them to tap out in English did you? It's German, all the way."

MEETING PEACH

1940

The rest of the morning was spent going over the Morse alphabet. First Nancy had been made to copy it out over and over in order. Then Miss Halsall had called out letters and numbers randomly and she had had to write them down. "No hesitation; hesitation is our enemy," Miss Halsall would say.

At 1 o'clock Nancy was taken back along the corridor and down the stairs. Men and women came streaming out of rooms all over the house. They all walked down the corridor, away from the front of the house, and out of a wide back door. The door led into more gardens and, glancing across, Nancy could see several wooden huts across an expanse of lawns, stretching out towards a dense area of trees. Nancy was glad of the sharp, cool air of outdoors. She would have liked to stop and fill her lungs but Miss Halsall was hurrying her along. "If you're not careful you can be queuing for your entire break and only get half a mug of cheap broth," she warned.

They came to a large hut on the edge of a field. On entering Nancy immediately noticed a long queue snaked across one wall. It was a canteen. They took their place at the back. Nancy glanced around her. Long tables had been set out in rows. Some were already full with men and women who were sat eating, talking and laughing. Some wore uniforms of varying colours but others were in plain clothes of brown, tweed trousers and knitted waistcoats. As she shuffled forwards in the queue Nancy could see women dressed in white standing in front of a row of large, steaming pots. A row of teapots had been perched on tables beside the serving area. Nancy began to wonder what they'd be eating at school today and if they'd missed her, if questions had been asked and if it would get back to her parents.

When they reached the head of the queue Nancy selected cold Spam. A woman with red, puffy cheeks slopped a portion of slushy, boiled potato onto her plate. After collecting a glass of water Nancy looked out across the sea of bobbing heads to find Miss Halsall but she was nowhere to be seen. Suddenly she felt someone tug sharply at her elbow. She swung round and came face-to-face with a tall, lively young man in uniform.

"Looking for someone?" he asked.

"Yes, yes, I was with Miss Halsall but she's disappeared."

"I can help you find her," he said.

He guided her away from the serving area. "Just look down the rows, that's the best way," he said. "He balanced his mug of tea on his plate and reached across to give her his hand. "The name's Peach: well, that's what everyone calls me around here. I don't much answer to anything else."

"I'm Nancy, Nancy Brown."

He leant in to whisper. "First rule: don't give out your surname." He pulled his head back and grinned down at her. "But you'll be fine; you must be good or you wouldn't be here."

"Yes, well I hope so; I'm training for…"

"Now, hold on: don't tell me that either. In fact, don't tell me anything. We don't tell each other anything here."

"But we're on the same side."

"There you go again!" said Peach, grinning even more. "There's no stopping you is there? Listen, I mean it: rule number one means you know nothing and say nothing, understood?"

At that moment something, or someone, caught his eye and he sprang back. "Well if it isn't the most beautiful woman in the Service – tell me, have you changed your mind about the House ball? It will be a riot you know!" Peach grinned at Miss Halsall, who returned a cold smile.

"Stop fraternizing with my charge or I'll have you on night duty for a month."

"Ma'am," said Peach in a loud voice, suddenly standing to attention, his right arm springing to salute. Several people at nearby tables looked around.

"Very funny," said Miss Halsall, leading Nancy away.

"Why is he called Peach?" asked Nancy.

"On account of his young looks and peachy skin, of course!" came the reply. "Mind you, he knows it too well. Too cocky by half."

After lunch they returned to the training room. Miss Halsall sat behind the Morse key once more and began to tap out combinations of letters and numbers while Nancy transcribed them. She copied the Morse code onto special sheets of paper which had lines and boxes.

There she would fill in details of the intercept: the date, time and the message itself.

The work was hard and Nancy's eyes began to sting with fatigue. What's more she was disappointed. She was desperate to know more about the spy ring but for now they were stuck with the routine alphabet. Finally she transcribed the first complete sentence of the day. It was in English but, as Miss Halsall would constantly remind her, the ones for real were in German. "Well that will only make the job harder for me," thought Nancy to herself.

"That's all for today," said Miss Halsall crisply at 5 o'clock. "You may go home, same time tomorrow."

She walked out of the front door and onto the gravel drive.

"Bet your brain's bursting isn't it?"

Nancy heard the voice she now recognised as belonging to the man called Peach. He was sat on a motorbike, putting a helmet on. "Nah, it's all right," she said.

"They all say that but they'll get to you in the end," he said grinning. "Fancy a spin? I can drop you home."

Nancy stumbled for an answer. "No thanks, my folks won't let me go on a motorbike," she said.

"Shame; another time, perhaps." And with that he started up the engine and pulled away, roaring down the drive.

THE SECOND AND THIRD DAYS

1940

Nancy's second day at Megg House was much like the first, a fog of letters and words. Miss Halsall rigorously tapped out message after message in Morse code and Nancy would race to transcribe them onto the thin paper sheets.

Day three was different. Walking into the training room in the morning, Nancy was surprised to see no papers or Morse keys on the desk. Miss Halsall was nowhere to be seen. She sat down and waited. No-one came so she waited some more. Eventually she heard footsteps approaching the room but the figure who opened the door wasn't Miss Halsall at all, it was the tall, thin man who had visited her house and the Guide night, the same one from the room above the shop, the day she had been recruited. He didn't introduce himself so she decided to call him Sir on account of his air of authority.

"Halsey isn't in today," he said. "Don't know why because she's supposed to be. There will be a reasonable explanation I expect. No matter, we have a job for you to do."

He turned and opened the door and beckoned Nancy out of the room and into the corridor. She followed him down the staircase and onto the ground floor. They crossed the hallway. Sir opened a door. In front of them was the large room Nancy had seen through the window that first morning. Like then it was full of people. Nancy turned to Sir.

"You mean to tell me that everyone here is listening out for German spies?" she asked.

She was surprised by the reply. "No, not all of them; only a few, in fact. We don't just listen for the Germans in the town: we listen to them all across Europe. Catching the spy ring is only a small part of the work here, but the spies are just as deadly as a German U-boat. If you ask me, our spy work here is not taken anywhere near seriously enough. There simply aren't enough of us working on the spy ring: that's why you're here, of course. And I hope you're not the last; we need many more like you."

A woman in a stiff uniform walked over to them.

"One of the new volunteers here to do her first intercept shift," said Sir.

"You'd better follow me," she said to Nancy. Nancy glanced behind to see Sir leave the room.

Nancy was led to a desk in the centre of a row in the middle of the room. She sat down on a small stool. A young man sat to her left and a woman to her right. Both were bent over pieces of paper, their fingers furiously writing down messages played into the headphones they wore.

The woman in charge handed Nancy her headphones and leant over towards a black box on the desk. "You'll know this is a receiver of course, but as it's your first go I'll choose the frequency for you," she said. She reached forward and switched the dial until it rested upon a particular number.

The headphones were new and stiff and they pushed into Nancy's ears. After only a few seconds she began to hear a faint hiss. She looked around her. The woman had walked away. She knew from her father that dialling into a radio frequency – the number she was given - was a delicate thing, needing careful attention, so she tweaked the dial herself. She hit more hiss, louder this time. Another nudge brought the muffled sound of a high-pitched woman's voice shrieking out what sounded like a love song over the background of a piano. The words were in a foreign language. The woman in charge walked slowly behind her, glancing over the interceptors and their sets on either side of her. She stopped at Nancy's station and motioned to ask if she could speak. Nancy raised her hand to show she was not in the middle of some delicate intercept.

"Quiet today then?" asked the woman.

"Yes, nothing except some sad song being belted out somewhere in Europe," said Nancy.

"Keep at it," said the woman, walking away.

Nancy looked back towards the set. There was something coming through. It was a low-pitched tone. It disappeared. Then it was back. She grabbed a pencil and made ready to take it down. Was it Morse? It had to be; what else sounded like that?

She turned the dial again, just a fraction. Again her instincts were correct, for now it was clear. She raised her left hand to get the attention of the supervisor and with her right hand she began taking down the dots and dashes. They spelled out a jumble of words she did not recognise. "German words of course," she reminded herself. The woman came walking down the row of tables and stopped over her shoulder but said nothing. She watched while Nancy spent the next two minutes taking down the message.

Immediately, when it was over, Nancy ripped the piece of paper off the pad and handed it to the supervisor. The woman pursed her lips. "Short enough transmission time, but clear enough," she said. "I timed it: two minutes. Not long enough for the vans to be sure, but they could have been on before you detected them. I have to let the huts know, and Number 10 of course."

The woman walked up to a desk and picked up a telephone. Nancy did not understand. Vans? Number 10? Is she calling the Prime Minister to tell him? And to think Sir said the spy work was not being taken seriously enough. A few minutes later Sir himself came into the room. He spoke to the woman at the desk for a moment before approaching Nancy where she sat.

"Topping work, Miss Brown," he said.

He went to say something else but was suddenly silenced by raised voices coming from outside, all talking quickly over each other. A man in uniform ran into the room. In his right hand he held a small piece of white paper. "Spotted Sir, definite signal, the vans are going out now!"

Sir sprang around and quickly followed the uniformed man out of the room. Nancy decided to follow them. Other men were talking in the hallway.

"We think we have a definite lead," said one of the men. "Two signals across the town; we think we've tapped into an exchange."

"We know; one of the new volunteers has just listened in, but only for two minutes and it's not long enough," replied Sir.

"We had them longer, Sir; this could be what we've been waiting for."

"Where's Peach? asked Sir. "Downstairs? No? Then get him on the phone!"

The man rushed into a room on the opposite side of the hallway. A moment later she could hear retreating footsteps and fading voices. For the second time that day she was alone and, again, she didn't know what to do. After a few minutes she sat down on a single chair by the open front door and waited. Every so often a man or woman in uniform would open one of the doors and cross the corridor before disappearing into another room. Eventually she saw Sir walking towards her. He motioned for her to follow him into a small office. The door outside had a printed sign with the words 'Wing Commander Henley-Williams'. At least she now knew his real name, but what a mouthful. 'Sir' was much better, particularly as everyone else seemed to be calling him that. He shut the door behind him, walked over to his desk and threw himself into a chair with a weary thud.

"You're young, so I have to tell you that you must not, under any provocation whatsoever, repeat any of what you've seen and heard today, is that clear?" he said. Nancy barely knew what 'provocation' meant.

He gazed out of the window. Following his line of sight, Nancy saw two large, black vans coming up the drive. They came to a stop outside the entrance to the house. Several plain-looking men got out, their expressions pinched and strained. There was a loud rap at the door. "Come in," he shouted.

A younger man, also in uniform, entered the room and saluted. "They're back, Sir. De-briefing in ten?"

"Yes, yes," said Sir, waving him away, before calling him back. "Tell one of the Wrens to take one of the cars and drive Miss Brown home," he ordered. He stood up. "Well Miss Brown, it seems you're one of the team now. Glad to have you on board and all that, but that's enough excitement for one day. Go home now and we will be in touch."

"Did you get them then?" asked Nancy.

He gave a small smile. "No, not this time." He turned to stare out of the window again. "It's important you know that we're not just listening to what they say, but we're tracking their signals to see if we can get to them before they disappear. Well today was one of those days, only they'd gone by the time we got there. Can't say I blame them." He signed heavily. "But we think the message is important and that takes us forward."

There was another pause. He turned back to look at her. "What shifts do you want me to do and what about school?" asked Nancy.

"Don't worry about that; we'll sort it out when we need to," he said with a wave of his hand. "You're good, that's the main thing, so we have to work the rest out."

They shook hands briefly before he led her from the room. A young Wren was waiting in the hallway.

ARTHUR

2010

Arthur Lane was aged twelve and lived with his mum, dad and older brother on a 1970s housing estate not far from Mr Smith's house. If he had an extraordinary talent it hadn't been noticed either at home or at school. Indeed, the only thing that marked him out was his virtual silence. Whereas other boys would speak or shout out loud in the classroom, Arthur would never raise his hand or even talk when he didn't have to. If he was asked a question in class he would often go red and quietly stutter out an answer, sometimes to the amusement of the other pupils.

No-one seemed to know where his chronic shyness had come from, especially as life at home was anything but quiet. Both his parents and older sibling, Michael, known as Micky, were outgoing, outspoken and even occasionally outlandish. If there were arguments, a heavy-handed crashing around the house, loud singing to the radio or shouting at the TV, Arthur would shrink down into his chair or slope off to his room for some peace and quiet. His soft and sensitive nature clashed with his family's rugged robustness. It also meant that he lacked the courage to quit his Saturday job at Mr Smith's.

One Saturday he got up quite early to leave for Mr Smith's house as usual.

"How much longer are you going there?" his mother had asked him as he was about to leave the house.

"Dunno, until Mr Pickles decides not," said Arthur.

"Seems like they've forgotten about you," she said. "I'll ring Mr Pickles today and mention it."

The short walk to Mr Smith's would take Arthur from his own estate and through the remains of the original village of Orethorpe. The route took him past the only old buildings, constructed many years ago when the then village had been small and quaint. Arthur had seen faded, black and white photographs in the parish magazine showing The Green and the road outside the post office, only then the roads were little more than dirt tracks. The images were soft and fuzzy, not at all like the crisp, hard lines of today's tarmac and pavements or the bright lights of the mini supermarket.

He always chose to go through The Green and not via the alternative route, which took him past a more modern row of shops. There, night and day, a group of several boys would regularly gather. Sometimes they'd be playing on their mobile phones; occasionally one of them would steal a few cigarettes from an adult and would stand around smoking proudly while most of the others looked on. Arthur dreaded their stares.

But this Saturday as he rounded the corner to cross The Green he was suddenly stopped by a sign saying the road was closed. Ahead of him he could see the tarmac had been dug up. Men were looking over a machine which let out a smell of burnt treacle. He had no choice but to turn right, past one of the pubs and a tiny row of old terraced houses. He felt a slight twist in his stomach as he rounded the next corner, which would bring him out at the shops. "I'll just keep my eyes down and walk fast," he promised himself.

At first he couldn't see anyone there but within half a minute he could see ahead of him the backs of a group of boys he knew, but wished he didn't. "At least they can't see me coming; I can just hurry past," he said to himself.

Suddenly one of the group swung round until he was facing him. "It's the last boy Scout, goody two shoes," he jeered.

Arthur gulped hard and continued walking. On reaching the group he glanced up.

"We want a light, you got one? Better still, go in and buy us some."

One of the boys was walking towards him. Arthur carried on walking but the boy followed. He was shouting now, jeering. He was walking faster, reaching Arthur. He was prodding him and then jutted out his foot, catching Arthur's shin. Arthur lost his balance and fell forward. He landed on the ground on his knees and let out a yelp of pain. The boys' jeers grew louder and they moved closer. Arthur managed to get to his feet. The main bully was standing next to him, goading him. Arthur glanced at him and at the others, now very close, and he began to run as fast as he could.

He ran all the way to Mr Smith's. The old man looked shocked to see the breathless, tearful boy at the front door. He took Arthur down the hallway and into the kitchen. Arthur slouched in a small chair beside a small kitchen table. Blood was trickling from one of his knees.

Mr Smith sat next to him and peered at his wounded leg. "Now then lad, let's take a look at you," he said, his head moving closer to Arthur's leg, his eyes squinting. Arthur felt the blood trickle reach his lower leg and watched as it stained his sock. The wound throbbed and he had begun to cry. Mr Smith staggered into the bathroom down the hall and returned with some toilet paper and a plaster. Both were slowly and gently applied in turn to the wound.

After a minute or so, and between sniffs, Arthur realised he could smell grease and soon realised it was coming from the cooker. He could see a white, ageing appliance with rusty-looking electricity rings. A stack of frying pans stood on the top. Tins were arranged in rows along a worktop and there was a deep, white sink of a kind he'd not seen before. A net curtain hung across a small window above the sink.

A plaster was applied and Arthur was given a piece of toilet roll to blow his nose. Mr Smith got up and went to an overhead cupboard. His eyes squinted more than usual as he groped around inside with his right hand. He retracted his hand, in which he grasped two delicate-looking cups stacked upon two saucers. "Here we are," he said wearily, placing them on the table.

The cups were white but someone had painted tiny blue flowers onto them. Mr Smith then turned to the large, bright green teapot by the window. His hand shook as he poured boiling water from the kettle into it before lifting it over to the table. His trembling hands struggled to hold the pot as he poured the weak, sandy-coloured liquid into the cup. A tiny jug held some milk which Mr Smith slopped into the cup. He handed the cup to Arthur. Arthur's big hands struggled to handle the delicate cup and his finger only just fitted into the handle. And he soon realised that a tiny cup with a saucer didn't hold anywhere near as much liquid as a mug because it only took three gulps to drain the entire contents.

Mr Smith stared down at his own hands. Each time he brought the cup to his mouth he would raise his eyes to Arthur before swallowing his tea loudly and lowering both his hands and eyes back to the table. Several minutes passed in silence.

"I hate this place," said Arthur eventually.

The old man looked up. "What do you mean?" he asked.

"I wish something happened around here, but it's always happening somewhere else," said Arthur, only half-knowing what he meant. "This place is pathetic and petty," continued Arthur, repeating words he'd heard his father and brother use.

With that Mr Smith chuckled. "You want a bit of excitement; well, be careful what you wish for," said the old man, lifting his cup to his lips again.

Another minute passed before Mr Smith spoke again. "There will always be bullies in this life, boy, always." He went to say something else but there was a loud rap at the front door. Mr Smith raised himself up and shuffled into the hallway. A short time later Arthur heard voices from the front door.

"I've finally tracked you down, Mr Smith," said a man's voice from outside. The voices continued.

"What newspaper did you say you were from?" he heard Mr Smith ask.

A moment later Arthur heard the sound of the front door close together with footsteps enter the living room.

Someone then shut the living room door. The voices were low and muffled but Arthur could hear some of what was being said. Odd words leaked through the walls, words such as "gazette", "files", "interview" and "classified". The door of the living room opened again and he heard the men emerge.

"If you want it in writing, Mr Smith, I will get my editor...."

"That won't be necessary," said Mr Smith, his voice slightly raised.

"But it's no longer official secrets, you know that, and soon we'll know even more," said the man.

"Well you may think that, young man: now, if I can say goodbye."

The wind must have caught the front door for it slammed shut. The old man shuffled back through to the kitchen. His face looked pained. Arthur quickly looked down at his cup. If there was any tea left in it he would have gulped it down.

"What a foolish notion," said Mr Smith in a half-whisper as he lowered himself back into his chair.

HOME

1940

Nancy's first few days of training were over. To her surprise she was not asked to return to Megg House at all that week. On the drive home with the young Wren she had been told to wait for further instructions on when to return, but was told it would be soon.

That Friday night the Luftwaffe came again. These were not the Germans that Megg House was straining to detect. These Germans *wanted* to be heard. They knew the noise of their engines, the air raid sirens and the bombs would send everyone scrambling for the nearest shelter. There, mothers would clutch their babies, men would strain to listen by the entrance and schoolchildren would crouch down, wanting it to be over. The German planes didn't just attack the homes, factories, roads and docks of their enemy, but their very hearts, their resolve, their courage and their fight. That's what their terror was for.

Crouched in the darkness inside their shelter in the yard, Nancy, Mary and their parents heard the first boom.

"Not close, thank the Lord," Mother had said.

Mary began talking of her supervisor at the draper's shop and the silly woman who kept trying to coax extra rations of cloth out of the owner. "She said there would soon be a revolt over the coupons, saying the clothes are poor quality and everyone needs more curtains and towels," she said.

"I hope Mr Delores gave her short shrift for being so selfish and rude," said Mother.

"He won't, he's too soft. Besides, he says she's a valued customer."

"No such thing as that these days, love; we're all in the same boat," said Father. He was sitting cross-legged next to his wife.

"Mrs Delores would've told her what's what," said Mother.

"Yes, but she's hardly there any more, she's so busy with her women's War group these days."

When the all-clear came Father ran inside and came out with a blanket. He wrapped it around Nancy's small frame and would have carried her inside had Nancy allowed him to. Back in her bedroom she made straight for the window and glanced down at the main street in front of her. The street lights were not on, of course, but she could make out a young man, no more than twenty. He was a volunteer dispatch rider, used to take messages between different people during a bombing. Nancy recognised the man as Jack Jones. He was lodging with the Harris family next door, although where they found the space for his bed she could not fathom. Her father was there too and the two men were talking, their faces bowed. A shiver worked its way up through her body and she got back into bed, wriggling down between the cold sheets.

The next morning there was a sharp rattle on the front door. It was Miss Jolly. She was dressed in her immaculately pressed Guide Captain uniform, her eyes gleaming. "Oh Nancy, I'm so glad to have caught you in. Is your mother at home?"

Nancy led her through the front room and into the kitchen where Mother was crouched over the table, clearing up the breakfast plates. Audrey, home from a night shift, sat reading the paper near the fire.

"Good morning, Mrs Brown. I wonder if I could borrow Nancy for a few hours?" Miss Jolly didn't wait for an invitation to speak.

Mother straightened herself up. "What do you need Nancy for?"

"Uphill was badly hit last night, I don't know if you've heard," replied Miss Jolly. She glanced at Nancy and lowered her voice until it was almost a whisper. "Four members of one family dead, only a couple of young children left."

"Dreadful," whispered Mother. Audrey put down her newspaper and stared at Miss Jolly.

"The Guides are doing their bit to help and we've been asked to go and see what we can do," said Miss Jolly.

"Haven't they got the Women's Voluntary Service for that?" asked Audrey.

"Oh yes, there are lots of WVS volunteers, but they always need more," said Miss Jolly. "We've been doing our special War badges for some months now to prepare us for a time like this, haven't we Nancy?"

Nancy didn't reply, but just looked from Miss Jolly to Mother.

"Take her if you want," said Mother with a wave of her tea towel. "Have her back before blackout, mind."

Ten minutes later Nancy and Miss Jolly joined the other Guides already at the scene. Crossing into Jerry

Road, Nancy could hear the shouts and squeals of children playing. Looking up, she could see them running and jumping among the concrete skeletons of the bombed-out homes.

Nancy and another Guide called Helen were assigned a spot opposite a row of bombed houses. Their floors were thick with dust, rubble, burnt pieces of wallpaper, charred furniture and broken glass. There were gaping holes in some of the walls fronting the street.

For several hours she and the others were kept busy handing out great mugs of boiling soup to weeping women and men in sooty clothes and with grey features. They wiped away the tears and dribbles from the babies and helped the families heap what possessions they had left into wheelbarrows and prams. At 3 o'clock Miss Jolly came over to them.

"You've been wonderful, girls, but probably time to push off home now," she said.

Released from her duties, Nancy said goodbye to the group. It was a relief to walk away from the white, shocked faces of the newly homeless.

The air was still, but damp. Strangers hurried past, the men's shoulders hunched and hats drawn down, the women holding scarves or handkerchiefs to their mouths to protect them from the pungent air. As she passed a café she spotted a man sat in a window seat, his head propped up against the glass. He was clearly asleep. The bombings had left people edgy but they had also left them exhausted. Recently she had caught herself searching the faces of strangers hurrying along the streets or dawdling in shop doorways. She would look from one to another, searching for any sign that they somehow didn't belong. Would she spot a spy if they fumbled with their money in a grocery shop, staring down at the unfamiliar coins; if they mispronounced a common greeting to the assistant or leant forward to reveal a foreign label in their clothes?

She wanted some time away to think about all that was happening, what she had been asked to do. She climbed a hill away from the town centre. It led to a small clearing and then wide, open fields. She had been here many times: flying kites with Father and Mary, playing hide and seek with Joyce, summer picnics with the Guides.

She turned around to face the town below her. In front of her was the dark bulk of the Granvilles factory, black smoke rising from its many chimneys. Thorpe and Price were in the valley to the left. She could not see Gobley and Sons from where she stood, but knew it stood behind her over the hill. Langleys, where Father and Audrey worked, was down the hill to her left, close to her school. All the factories were full of the thousands of new people who had moved into Orethorpe to work for the War effort. The factory buildings had been extended, new ones added, like the rows of huts in the grounds of Megg House. Like there, the factory workers were not allowed to say what they were doing or what exactly the factories were producing.

She walked a little further and found a bench but as she sat down the first cold splashes landed on her. She looked up. It had begun to rain. Within a minute it was hard, proper rain. She got up and began to rush down the hill again. On reaching the town she turned towards the Three Tuns café, its homely lights spilling out onto the grey pavement.

THE CAFÉ

1940

On opening the door Nancy was hit by a wall of people's backs. The one large room of the café was packed with bodies. A line of trench and tweed overcoats, boiler suits and uniforms topped with the gleaming, short hair of the men and the tightly curled hair of the women, stretched in front of her. Steam rose from their damp clothes, mixing the musty smell of cloth with the aroma of coffee.

Every available chair was taken by factory workers finished after their Saturday shifts and military men and women with weekend passes. Those who were left to stand were crowded around the small tables. In the distance Nancy could hear the bell of the till sound every few seconds, the clang of metal coins in the tray and the heavy drawer being shoved back into its slot. Men were talking loudly into each other's ears. A woman across the room shrieked with laughter.

She turned to leave but as she began to reach for the door handle it was opened from the other side. Suddenly she was face-to-face with Audrey. Nancy was just about to say something when she noticed a hand around her sister's waist. A man had appeared at her side.

"Nancy love, what are you doing here, I thought you were out with the Guides?" said Audrey, a tang of irritation in her voice.

"We've finished for the day," replied Nancy.

"This is Joseph, a colleague from the factory." The older sister gestured to the man at her side.

"Supervisor if you don't mind, love," he said with a snort.

"This is my sister, Nancy."

"Pleased to meet you I'm sure. Just as good-lookin' as your Sis, eh? Must run in the family!"

Audrey pretended to prod him in the ribs.

"Oh be quiet!" she said.

"Do you want to join us?" he asked.

"No thanks; I'm just leaving."

Joseph simply smiled and guided Audrey around the tables to the right. Nancy looked after them and it was then that she thought she saw someone else she recognised. It was Tom. He was seated on a window sill in the nearest corner of the room and smiled up at her. "You all right then?" he said, a note of excitement in his voice.

"Just trying to dodge the rain like everyone else," she replied.

"You want me to fetch you anything," he said. Before she had a chance to reply he'd sprung up and was squeezing his small frame through the throng. Nancy took his place in the corner. A few minutes later a steaming mug appeared in front of her eyes. "It's not full as they're running out but it's better than nothin', eh?" said Tom.

"Ta, I'll pay you back," said Nancy.

"Don't be daft," he said.

She took a sip of the weak, brown liquid. It tasted as bland as it looked.

"I'll wait until it slackens off and then make a run for it," said Tom.

They passed several minutes in silence. Nancy's eyes constantly moved across the room. Jack Jones, the young man lodging with the Harris family next door, was sat at a table on the other side of the room. At 20 he was almost twice Nancy's age and they'd never said a lot to each other. He pulled his coat around his shoulders and made for the door. Nancy watched him go before she glanced over towards the counter and saw someone else that she recognised. It was Miss Temple, a new teacher from school. One morning in assembly she'd been made to stand in front of the entire school and be introduced. She barely looked older than Mary. Later Father had told her it was because all the young male teachers were getting ready to be called up.

Miss Temple stood to one side of the counter, holding a mug. A man stood by her side. At first the pair stood alone but when she glanced up another time Nancy saw that they'd suddenly been joined by another couple. Miss Temple looked slightly irritated at the intrusion. Her faint smile was frozen and her frame had stiffened. The man with her didn't appear to have noticed. He began waving his arm for the assistant on the other side of the counter to come and serve them. He shook hands with the new man, all the time chattering on.

"I said, is everything alright at home?"

Nancy swung her head back towards Tom. "What did you say?" she asked.

"I said, is everything all right at home?"

"Yes, yes," said Nancy, taking another sip.

"Horrible stuff isn't it? They say it's Bovril but of course it's not. Wouldn't be surprised if it's boiled mud off the potatoes."

Half an hour passed. Occasionally Nancy would glance over to the windows to watch the rain, but soon they were too steamed up to see anything at all. Tom continued to talk but she barely noticed. The minutes passed and the rain began to ease. People began to leave the café. Nancy waited until it was almost empty before she got up to leave.

Miss Temple and the man were still at the café counter. As she walked towards them the man suddenly swung around to say something to the couple behind them, but he lost his balance and stumbled forward. The coffee in his cup splashed onto Nancy's coat. "Oh excuse me, excuse me," he said, regaining his balance.

Miss Temple reached out her hand. It held a napkin for Nancy.

"I'm okay, it's nothing," said Nancy, using the napkin to soak up the liquid.

"I'm so clumsy, I really am."

Nancy looked up with a smile. Her eyes caught Miss Temple. "Nice to see you again, Miss," she said.

"You're at King Edward's, then, I haven't come across you yet." Miss Temple glanced over towards the man. "The school I'm now working in," she said in explanation.

"Yes; yes, but I've seen you in assembly," said Nancy. "Well, the rain is easing so I'm going now; don't worry about the coat."

Tom was waiting for her by the door. "Friends of yours?" he asked.

"A new school teacher."

"And with a clumsy clot by the look of it," said Tom.

"He just slipped," replied Nancy.

By now they were outside. She went to say goodbye but was surprised to see him smiling. "What's up?" she said.

"Someone's waiting for us, that's what," he said.

Glancing across the street Nancy saw Peach leaning against a large car. He glanced up as they approached.

"Small world, well, small town anyway," he said. He was unsmiling, almost scowling.

Tom went to say something but was stopped by the sudden wail of the air raid siren. Everyone paused a moment before Peach lurched forward and made for the driver's door of the car. "Two air raids in two days, Megg House will be worried," he said, reaching out for the catch of the door. He glanced up at them. "Hadn't you better be off before someone misses you?"

Tom spoke up. "Megg House will miss us the most if they're worried, won't they?"

Peach let out a snort. "I'm sure we can cope," he said. But then he hesitated. "On second thoughts, maybe you could be of use. Everyone's worn out after last night's action. Get in if you want." He cocked his head at both Nancy and Tom. Tom didn't need to be told twice. He opened the back door and flung himself inside, motioning for Nancy to follow him.

She had only just climbed into the car when it hastily pulled out into the road. Soon they were speeding away, past the rows of tightly-packed houses and out towards Megg House.

NUMBER 10

1940

The car swung into the drive in front of Megg House. A Wren was standing at the front door peering up towards the skies. She saluted Peach as he approached. "They're downstairs," she said.

"Thank you," replied Peach, brushing past her.

Nancy and Tom followed him into the hallway, but instead of turning left towards Sir's office or the Intercept Room, where Nancy had carried out her first shift, he twisted right and into one of the large rooms across the hall. Unlike the others it was not full of desks and working radio sets but had sofas and easy chairs, a fireplace and a well-stocked bookshelf. Peach approached an alcove in a side wall. A moment later Nancy saw the wood panelling reveal a door. Peach disappeared inside. "Everyone down into Number 10," he shouted back towards them.

Nancy, accompanied by Tom, walked through the door and realised that a narrow, stone staircase was facing her. She carefully walked down. At the bottom her eyes began to blink in the artificial lighting. Ahead of her two narrow corridors branched away. Bare light bulbs connected by wire had been pinned up against the brickwork, their glow bouncing off the whitewashed walls and ceiling.

"This way, follow me," Peach said to them over his shoulder. They passed several doors. Each one had a number, some had signs: 'Clerks', 'Typists', 'Boardroom', 'Night-Shift Dorm'. Everywhere she looked men and women in uniforms were streaming out of the doors and into the corridor, following her, pushing her deeper into the underground maze. They hurried to the end of the corridor and took a sharp turn to the right. Another wall of white bricks hemmed them in. Nancy noticed a man in uniform stationed outside a set of double doors. He stepped aside as they approached.

Peach beckoned Nancy through the doors. It was a scene of colour and chaos. Maps, papers, telephones and the constant movement of uniforms around the room swirled in front of her eyes.

Nancy took several steps forward and realised she was standing on some sort of upper deck, the rest of the room sweeping out several feet below. A table to the left dominated the area and was strewn with lined papers, letters, drawings and maps. All were held down by discarded pencils, tin mugs and notepads. The table also contained a row of brightly painted telephones. A printed label had been attached to each one: 'ARPs', 'Police', 'Coastguard', 'DF unit' and 'Filter Room'. Each time one of the telephones rang, a young Wren would sprint up to it to answer, hastily taking a message.

Suddenly she was buffeted by the movement of more uniforms sweeping into the room and Nancy was almost forced down the steps. Everyone was crowding around the centre, looking down on something she couldn't immediately see. She walked up to the crowd and, after several minutes, managed to nudge her way through to the front. What she saw astonished her. It was a large map on an even bigger table. But it wasn't a map of Europe, or even of England: it was a map of Orethorpe. The streets had been carefully plotted in black; the roofs and spires of the Catholic and Anglican churches had been drawn and the shops were clearly marked by name. Even the railway line running from the countryside, past the factories, through the town and back into the countryside had been carefully drawn.

"Where on earth are we?" she asked.

"Number 10," shouted Peach from the other side of the map table.

"You mean like Number 10 Downing Street?" asked Nancy.

"Not quite, love; you'll have to go to London to see that," someone said in her ear.

Peach looked up. "This is *our* Number 10."

It was then that Nancy noticed Sir. He was already standing over the map table. A man in uniform stepped forward.

"It's probably just another random raid, Sir."

"It's more than that."

Several women in Wren uniforms were poised over the map. Each wore a set of headphones and held a long wooden stick in their hands. Nancy and the others watched for several minutes as they skillfully pushed wooden blocks across the map, using the sticks.

"They're plotting the raid," said Tom in her ear. Nancy hadn't realised he was standing beside her.

"Why are they wearing headphones?" she whispered back.

"They get told the coordinates by the other stations," he replied. "The German planes are tracked and we're told if they're heading our way."

The noise in the room had lowered as everyone sat or stood studying the young Wrens moving the delicate wooden blocks across the board. First the blocks came to rest on the edge of the town but within a few minutes they had been slid across the outlying streets and came to rest over the area which was home to the Granvilles and Thorpe and Price factories. Nancy remembered how, earlier that day, she had looked over towards the factories herself. Something inside her shuddered.

"It's the factories, Sir," said a young man in uniform.

Sir looked up. "Anti-aircraft guns?"

"Deployed, Sir, but unsuccessful so far."

Nancy knew that anti-aircraft guns had been dotted around the town, ready to shoot down enemy aircraft if they approached. Her heart sank at the thought that the guns' firepower had only shot off harmlessly into the night air, leaving the German planes to continue on their way.

"And the RAF?" asked Sir.

One of the Wrens pulled down her headphones and looked across to answer him. "They're already up there, Sir."

"By golly, there's to be a dogfight then," said Tom. "By gosh, how I want to be out there watching it."

"What do you mean?" asked Nancy. "Are they sending the RAF up to shoot them down?"

"What else can they do, it's either them or us."

Suddenly a telephone on the upper table began to ring, followed by another and then another. The brief spell had been broken and, once again, the room erupted

71

into noise. The uniformed men and women crowded around the map dispersed, apart from Sir, Peach and the Wrens. Nancy and Tom also stayed where they were.

Peach looked towards Sir. "Why send in spies if they're planning to wipe us out from the air?" he asked.

Sir looked up. "They need to know if we're worth it, what we're actually doing here and how important Orethorpe is to the War effort." He pointed to where the wooden plotting bars had been placed on the map. "Look, they're already getting more targeted. How else would they know the factories are there?"

There was another pause before one of the Wrens looked up. "The RAF have engaged the enemy, Sir," she said.

"How many of them?"

"The enemy, Sir?"

"Them and us."

"Five German planes and three of ours, so far, Sir."

Nancy felt a tug at her sleeve. It was Miss Halsall. "Come on, you're no use to us here, why not help with the intercepts upstairs?" she said.

"Good idea," barked Sir from across the table. "Keep your chin up and your head on your shoulders," he added.

Nancy was led from the room. Glancing back she saw that Tom had not moved from his spot. She still had no idea what he actually did for Megg House and no-one, especially not him, would tell her.

She was led back down the corridor and up the stairs. Walking into the Intercept Room she saw the usual rows of desks and radio sets. Older men and women walked between the rows. Every so often one of the interceptors would raise a hand and the superior officers would go over to them to be handed a completed intercept log. Several younger officers stood by the door to receive the logs. "Presumably to take straight down to Sir," thought Nancy.

She was given a seat in front of a new-looking set. As before, the tight, new spring on the headphones banged the set against her ears. She was handed a sheet of paper. On it someone had written a number. "The frequency you're to monitor," said one of the supervisors.

Nancy turned the dial of the radio set. The hum of the other sets in the room suddenly clouded her ears. She closed her eyes. All that came through her headphones was the usual hiss. As on her first intercept, she turned the dial this way and that. Several minutes passed, then several more. She strained to hear. Another ten minutes came and went, then another ten, then another. She had been seated for almost forty minutes when she heard it. It was no more than a sparrow of a noise, a tiny, bird-like tapping, hopping along the radio band frequency like one of those small creatures skipping along a washing line.

She began to make out the dits and dots and furiously wrote them down on the pad in front of her. The message was long, longer than before. Nancy realised that it was the same message, over and over. It was repeated four or five times before it came to an abrupt end. Nancy raised her hand and the supervisor was there in a moment. She reached out her hand to take the paper log from her but, at that moment, Nancy jumped from her seat

"I want to take it down to him," she said.

She ran out of the room, across the corridor and into the empty room. A minute later she was handing the sheet to Sir inside Number 10. He read it slowly then looked up. "Do you know what it says?" he asked.

"I think so, it's the same message over and over," said Nancy. "It's from a spy, I know it is. They're panicking because they're being bombed. Look, it's in German. It says *why now, why now*" and, look here, *'too soon, too soon'*.

A phone began to ring and a Wren quickly picked it up. "Bomber Command for you, Sir," she shouted across.

"Tell them I'll call back from my office," came the reply. He walked over to the stairs and galloped up them two at a time.

The dog fight was over within the hour. One German plane had been hit and limped off, smoke coming from the rear end, according to Peach. The others had been chased out of the area, but had not, as far as anyone knew, been destroyed.

Shortly after they were given the all-clear, Sir reappeared inside Number 10. He walked over towards Nancy. "I want you to stay on for a short while," he said. "Do your intercepts from here and learn what you can. We may be asking you to do something for us."

"But what about Mum and Dad and school?" she asked.

"It's only for a few days and you're not required to stay overnight," he replied. "I'll sort the rest. Your Guide work is a good cover."

"But I thought you were just listening to the radio messages," said Nancy.

"We are. What do you think all those uniforms upstairs are doing? We're listening to the enemy both here and overseas, but down here, well, down here the job is to find these spies. And we're not the only ones. We've even got civilians at it: listening at all hours behind their radio sets. "Voluntary Interceptors" we call them: VIs for short."

"But why can't we find them? How hard can it be in a town this size?"

"Harder than you think when they move like shadows."

He walked over towards the map.

"Not much damage, Sir, considering," said Peach. "The RAF gave them a good fright."

"Well it's the first time we've had them and that's only because the 'top brass' is finally starting to realise we need air cover as much as anything else," said Sir. He turned back towards Nancy. "Come over here Miss Brown, you need to hear this."

Sir handed a piece of paper to Peach. Peach read it in silence. "An intercept, Sir?" he asked.

"Yes, tonight, during the raid. Miss Brown intercepted it, as did several others."

Peach looked down at the message again. "It sounds like whoever sent this is afraid," he said.

"Precisely, and what does that tell you?"

"Well it says it here, Sir, 'too soon'."

"Exactly."

"What's too soon?" asked Nancy.

"That," said Sir, "is the question. I would guess that the ringleader of the spies is not ready yet. His plan, whatever it is, has not been finalised and his men on the ground are not fully trained." Turning back to Peach he

75

continued, almost thinking aloud. "They parachuted in weeks ago, so what have they been planning all that time?" That is what we have to find out and find out quickly."

Returning to face Nancy, Sir added: "You have a remarkable talent for finding yourself at the centre of things Miss Brown. Thanks to your intercept you're as up to speed as we are. We must find this ringleader. If we find him the others will be scattered and without a proper plan. He's the key to this whole business, you could rightly say that he is the most dangerous spy of all."

FRIENDSHIP

2010

By July Arthur and Mr Smith were firm friends. What had started out as a weekly chore had become the highlight not only of the old man's week, but Arthur's as well. Ever since the day of his injury Arthur had always been invited in to eat and drink. Often Mr Smith would persuade him to eat some bread and butter or something on toast. "You know you really should have something; we don't want you fainting on the way home, do we?" he'd say, his voice vague but his eyes smiling.

Arthur had become used to sitting around the crumb-laden kitchen table. He no longer thought twice about the thin layer of dust on his baked beans or the faint crunch of grit from his slab of bread. He'd drink weak cups of tea with tiny shavings of paint that had come away from the ceiling or the soapy taste of washing up liquid that hadn't been rinsed away properly. Neither of them liked to talk very much, so these simple meals would often pass in virtual silence.

But then the newspaper reporter returned. Arthur was working in the garden at the time. The young man, dressed in a suit, stood beside the front door. "It's all declassified now, Mr Smith," he said. "This is an opportunity to celebrate what you did, what you all did."

"I'm not interested, thank you," said Mr Smith. He went to shut the door but the reporter leant in.

"No-one blames you lot for what happened, if that's what you're worried about. We weren't the only ones: look at Coventry and Sheffield. No-one could have stopped those either. But this is a side of the War we've never known about before."

The door slammed. Arthur watched the reporter walk down the path. The boy turned to him. "What do you want him for?" he asked.

The reporter stopped. "We want to know about his War experiences," he replied.

"Why: 'cos he's so old?"

The reporter chuckled. "He's a lot more than that, or at least he was." He glanced back towards the house. "By the look of him he hasn't got much longer to tell his story, and there aren't many left to tell it either."

Arthur didn't know what he meant.

INTERCEPTS

1940

Nancy's introduction to Number 10 had been sudden, but she was not invited back down into the basement at Megg House for some time. Instead, each day, she would climb the hill and walk up the drive to carry out her intercepts from the ground-floor Intercept Room. Sometimes the messages came, but mostly they did not and her shift would be a waste.

The messages that *did* come were on the same frequency as before. Sometimes they would come suddenly, a hastily tapped scribble before the nervous operative yanked off their headphones and quickly shut down the machine. Sir had told her that the signals could be tracked by 'the vans', the same ones she had seen on the day of her first intercept. They could, somehow, trace the signal and even find out where it was coming from. Such detection would mean a house raid and perhaps an arrest of one of the spies in the town.

"They know this of course, they know we can trace them," Sir had told her. "That's why they're only on for a few minutes, if that, at a time. Then they pack up their kit and move on, quickly."

"Why take the risk at all?" Nancy had asked.

"Well, they don't most of the time, but sometimes it's essential that they report back or ask for more orders," he'd replied. "Don't forget that they're here to gather information about what we're doing as much as anything."

"So the Germans know where to send the bombers?" Nancy had continued.

"Precisely," Sir had said, adding: "and other things besides."

Each day, before she left Megg House, Nancy would be handed an envelope telling her when she would be required the following day. Once she was also handed a letter addressed to her parents. "It explains that you've been chosen for some special emergency evacuation training, first-aid, that sort of thing," she was told by a young man in uniform.

That evening Nancy handed the letter to Mother after tea. She read it quickly and handed it to Father.

"It says you're going up to that big house on Manor Road to do special training: so that's what they do up there, is it?" asked Mother.

Nancy almost choked on her drink. What were they doing writing down the name of Megg House? "Oh I don't know; boring stuff as usual, I bet," she said, her face reddening.

"Mary says that Mrs Delores knows another woman who knows someone working there. They've been billeted with her, only she's not allowed to ask any questions about it, that's what Mrs Delores says."

"It can't be that secret if they're letting the Guides in, Mother," said Nancy.

"Well just don't let them take advantage of you," said Mother.

"Your mother's right, Nancy: you've got your school work and your safety to think of," said Father. "If it gets too much I'll write back."

"It's fine, Dad," she mumbled in response.

JOYCE'S HOUSE

1940

"The Rolls is coming for us today, isn't that nice?" said Joyce with a gleeful grin. She delivered the news as they were coming out of school one day. It was Friday, the day Nancy usually went to her friend Joyce's for tea in the house next door to her family's. Sometimes, as a treat, Joyce's Father would finish work early and pick them up in his Ford car. It wasn't a real Rolls Royce, but they still referred to it as if it was and it was the family's pride and joy. Normally, Nancy loved to ride in it but today was to be different, for she was expected up at the House for an intercept debrief. She turned to Joyce. "There's something I've got to do first. I'll have to walk over: sorry."

"I thought you were coming for tea?" said Joyce.

"I am, I am, but I've an errand to run first. It won't take long. I'll be there for 5 o'clock, I promise."

Joyce shrugged and turned away in what looked like a sulk.

The debrief was only short and it was before 5 o'clock when Nancy rattled on the front door of Joyce's house.

"Well, nice of you to grace us with your presence, I'm sure." Mrs Harris met her at the door with her wide smile. She was a large, puffy lady and Nancy had never seen her without red cheeks and a scruffy, white apron. Tufts of fair hair had escaped an untidy bun.

"I'm so sorry, Mrs Harris," said Nancy quickly.

"Well, you're here now." She ushered Nancy inside. The Brown and Harris families were next door neighbours and their houses were exactly the same. But unlike her own home, with its small, neat efficiency, everything here was untidy and boisterous. She'd just stepped inside when Joyce approached her, also with a smile. She appeared to have forgotten her earlier sulk.

Within minutes other children had appeared from every corner of the house until a party of eight of them, including Mr and Mrs Harris, had gathered around the table. Nancy loved the clamour and noise, but most of all she loved seeing Kep, short for Keiren. He was the oldest of the Harris brood and an RAF pilot. He was also engaged to be married to Nancy's older sister, Mary. Where his family were loud, he was gentle. His soft voice and kindly manners clashed against their brashness. He had always been ready with a kind word for Nancy. He'd ask about her school work, admire her knitting and happily eat her first attempts at baking. At night he would sit by the fire with Mary and chat to Mother and Father about his family, the RAF, the schools he'd gone to and the people he knew. Since her introduction to Number 10, Nancy had often wondered if he had been one of the pilots sent up to defend the town. She dared not ask.

Today Kep sat across the table from Nancy but was almost completely engaged in talking to Jack Jones, the family lodger. Finally Kep turned to her. "Your mother tells me you're very busy doing relief work with the Guides."

"Yes, yes," Nancy hesitated. Even though she had been caught up in the world of Megg House she still struggled with the secrecy she was ordered to observe. Her natural defence had been to say as little as possible, but today Kep went on.

"She says you've even been invited up to the big house on the hill for training, is that right?"

Nancy's pulse quickened. "Yes."

Suddenly Jack Jones butted in. "Everyone is very curious as to what's going on up there," he said.

"Oh it's nothing; well, not nothing, just a bit of extra training, just in case," said Nancy. She had begun to feel her face redden.

"No chance of getting me in for a tour then?" said Jack with a grin.

"I'm afraid not."

"I'm surprised you've not been up there yourself as you're a dispatch driver," said Mrs Harris to Jack.

"Oh we're very lowly, just there to deliver the messages to the people that really matter," replied Jack. "Not like Miss Brown here, obviously. So tell me, who's based up there then? It might help me to know if it's ever bombed and I have to relay information on to the authorities, to help out and everything." He smiled while he spoke.

"I couldn't tell you," said Nancy. "We Guides are less important than anyone," she added. She got up to leave. "I'm sorry Mrs Harris but I haven't seen Mother all day and she may have something for me to do for her."

"I'll come too as I promised Mary I would pop in," said Kep.

They went through the Harrises' kitchen, into their back yard and out into a small alleyway that ran along the back of the row of houses. Stepping into her own yard Nancy saw the lights on in Father's shed. Lately she had noticed the creases on his forehead deepen and the dark shadows appearing underneath his eyes. She peered through the small window and saw him bent over another of his wireless radio sets. She could not stop because Kep had his hand under her arm to guide her in the dark and they carried on walking up to the back door of her house.

THE VANS

1940

"Nancy, can I have a moment?" The voice came from one of the Intercept Room supervisors. Nancy looked up. "They want you across the hall in ten," said the supervisor before walking away.

She took off the headphones and got up. The room across the hall was packed. Nancy could see a crowd of people crammed around a desk covered with maps. Sir was shouting out orders using words like 'bearing' and 'direction'. Nancy had no idea what he meant but she could see the others listening closely. Finally the crowd was dismissed with the usual "good luck". Everyone began to make their way out of the room. As the room emptied, Tom came over to her. "Finally, a big push tonight; you looking forward to it?" he asked.

"What big push?" Nancy replied.

"We're finally going out to try to catch them while they're at it, that's what," said Tom. "Good job an' all. They're up to something, we know that."

They walked across the room and out of the back door leading onto the rear lawns.

"They're sending the vans out," said Tom. "If they can lock on a radio signal from a spy and if they're close enough they've a chance of catching them at it, don't you see?"

"How can they do that?" asked Nancy.

Tom leant over. "If they get a strong enough signal they use two vans to lock onto it, then they can work together to plot the signal on a map to see where it's coming from. You'll understand when you see it in action."

"But why tonight?"

"I'm not sure, but I overheard someone saying that secret intelligence indicates that something is up."

They walked across the lawns and towards two large vans. Peach was standing beside one of them. "Good luck fellas, see you on the other side," he shouted to the people, including Tom, climbing into one of the vans. A couple shouted back in return. Peach opened the back of the other van and beckoned Nancy inside. Inside was a single, low table and several wooden stools. The table held three plain-looking boxes, all black. Peach swung inside behind her and took his place in front of one of the boxes. He reached out and sprung open a lid. The black box opened up and he reached inside for a pair of headphones and put them over his ears. Next he leant over and retrieved a piece of rolled paper from his rucksack. He unfurled it to reveal a map of Orethorpe. It was placed in the centre of the table. Next, Miss Halsall and a man in a Home Guard uniform climbed inside the van. Miss Halsall smiled at Nancy and went to sit on a stool opposite Peach. The Home Guard officer settled opposite Nancy. Both the new occupants of the van opened their boxes. Nancy saw Miss Halsall pull a Morse key out of her box. Soon all were wearing headphones.

"What's all this for?" asked Nancy.

"Huff-duff," said Peach with another grin.

"What on earth's that?"

"Huff-Duff, otherwise known as high-frequency direction finding," he said. "Finding the enemy, that's what."

"Test signal coming in now," said Miss Halsall to Peach.

"Someone's finally doing some work, eh?" said Peach with a grin. Nancy wondered if he was ever serious.

"Coming through clear enough," she said. Nancy saw she wasn't taking note of the message. "Quite as we expected," said Miss Halsall. "I'll radio through to the hut now, telling them we have it."

Miss Halsall leant forward to adjust the frequency dial in her box before she began tapping out her own Morse message on the key to her side. A minute or so later she looked up. "Message from No 10: we're cleared to proceed."

"Right you are," said Peach. Suddenly he was banging on the partition separating him from the van driver. An equally loud knock came back. Nancy heard the engine being started up and a moment later the van pulled away. The back window had been painted black with what looked like broad strokes of tar, but Nancy could just make out the dark form of the other van following them.

Miss Halsall appeared to be staring at the black dial on the box in front of her. The van bobbed up and down the uneven drive of Megg House and into the road. It turned right and it wasn't long before it was braking on the way down Conscience Hill. They were making their way into the centre of town. Looking out of the back window Nancy saw the other van sprint away in a different direction. Upon reaching level ground again she could just make out the outline of a third van parked beside a row of dark-bricked houses.

They came to the Market Square. The sound of the tyres hitting the cobbled stones sent a juddering, rattling sensation through the van, making the table tremble. When they came to the other side Nancy felt the van swing right, and out of the window she saw the signs and shutters of Pawnshop Passage. It was by far the narrowest road off the square, with just enough room for a single vehicle.

They soon came to the end of the passage and turned another right. Less than a minute later they came to a stop. Peach, Miss Halsall and the Home Guard remained hunched over their boxes. There was a sharp rattle on the back door. Peach nodded at the Home Guard, who reached over and turned the handle. A man Nancy didn't recognise bounced into the van. He shut the door behind him. "Rather cosy in here, yes?" he said. With no spare stools he crouched down on the floor between Nancy and the Home Guard.

"I hope none of us will get too comfortable before we're through," said Peach.

The new man wore a heavy, dark overcoat of high-quality wool together with a military hat. He turned to Nancy and smiled kindly. "Fancied a ride, did you?" he said.

Just then Peach interjected. "If you're looking to make yourself useful you can go and tweak the antenna as this sounds hissy," he said.

"This one too," said Miss Halsall. The Home Guard also nodded in agreement.

"No rest, eh?" said the man, smiling again. He turned around and opened the van door again to allow himself out.

The cold air blasted through the van. Nancy drew her coat closer around her. She heard banging and twisting sounds coming from the roof before the man climbed in again, slamming the door behind him.

They sat in virtual silence, the unnamed man with his back to the door and legs sprawled out under the table, Nancy staring out of the back window and the other three concentrating hard on their headphones and black dials. Occasionally, one of the three would look up and mutter something to each other about the frequency or the interference. The air was filling up with a burning, metallic smell.

Time passed slowly. Nancy sat hunched over the lapels of her coat. In time she felt her head bob down and her eyes closing until a woman's voice brought her back.

"Message from number two van: they've got something."

"What frequency?" replied Peach.

"I'm just asking now," said Miss Halsall, tapping into her Morse key. A few moments later she quickly scribbled something down on the pad in front of her. She tore off the paper and handed it to Peach. "The frequency," she said.

All three of them turned their dials and leant into their sets as if to shorten the distance between them and the longed-for clue. It was another minute before the man in the Home Guard uniform let out a loud exclamation. "I have it!" he shouted.

"What does it say?" cried Peach.

"It's very faint, but it could be them all right." said the Home Guard. "It's in German."

"Get it plotted, man."

He turned to Miss Halsall.

"Tell them we're plotting it now – what do they have?"

"They're just checking it now," she said.

"What on earth are they doing?" exclaimed the Home Guard.

"What is it, man?" said Peach.

"The signal is erratic." The Home Guard reached over to his set and began moving the dial.

"Don't lose them now man," shouted Peach.

He stood up to lean over the map on the table. The Home Guard man also leant over the table and began drawing a line across the map. "This is the line the signal is taking," he said.

"It could be anywhere along this line," said Peach. He looked over to Miss Halsall. "What do the others have? We need to know now."

The Home Guard man had begun to sweat and Nancy saw his Morse finger was trembling. He looked up to his superior with pleading eyes. "I keep losing them, they're erratic, perhaps deliberately."

Peach looked over towards Miss Halsall. "We need those coordinates now, tell them," he said, his voice raised.

"It's coming through now," she said.

Again she began to scribble down a list of letters and numbers on a piece of paper. Without bothering to wait Peach leant over and ripped the paper away from the pad. He and the Home Guard man began to draw another line across the map. The black ink swept over Granvilles factory, over the terraced streets, the shops and churches until it collided with the other line they had drawn earlier. The two streaks of black came together at Graves End Wood.

"They're at Graves End, message these coordinates now," cried Peach towards Miss Halsall. He turned to the Home Guard. "Message Megg House now, order all units to these coordinates." Both began to furiously Morse their vital messages through.

Moments later Nancy heard the engine start up and they began to move. The van bumped up and down as it raced through the narrow streets, jolting everyone inside. Minutes later the van was brought to an abrupt halt and its engine coughed and spat as the key was turned off and the back doors flung open. Nancy could see that they had arrived at the wood. Peach and the other man immediately jumped out. Peach turned around and shouted towards Nancy. "You're to stay here, you understand?" he said. Then, without waiting for her to respond, he was off. Miss Halsall and the Home Guard man remained stooped over their boxes and Morse keys, but outside the van it was all noise and clatter. More engines were drawing up, doors were being flung open and slammed shut, people were running, orders were being barked, yet, within a few minutes, all was quiet. Nancy leant out of the back door. A thick, steamy fog now covered the black woodland, making it impossible to see where the hunters had gone.

"Get back in here and shut the door," the Home Guard officer growled at her.

Nancy was reaching for the door handle to close it when the gunshots began. Two rang out in the distance, then another: closer this time. The Home Guard officer instantly rushed towards the door and jumped out. He quickly disappeared into the gloom. Miss Halsall, however, remained at her post, her Morse key furiously tapping. "Megg House will be hearing of the events almost as they happen," thought Nancy.

BANG! There was another gunshot, nearer this time. Nancy was suddenly very afraid, but she was also overcome with the urge to see what was happening. She leant forward, opened the doors a fraction and stole a glance outside. All she could see was the blurred orbs of the men's torches bobbing up and down in the fog, but she could hear the sound of frantic chasing and shouting. Minutes later the fuzzy outline of a man emerged from the dense obscurity of the woodland. He was running, but also springing from side to side, to avoid the scattered gunfire which was accompanied by frantic shouts of "don't lose him". Nancy suddenly realized that he was coming towards the van.

"He's here, he's here!" she shouted to Miss Halsall who immediately got up from her chair and went over to the door. The man was now much closer and would reach them in less than a minute. Miss Halsall leant forward to slam the door shut, but, at that moment, the man's body and face came clearly into view. Nancy gasped with the violent jolt of recognition. It was the man from the café, the one with Miss Temple, her schoolteacher!

Nancy bolted upright and flung open the door of the van before Miss Halsall could react. Less than a second later she was outside, facing his direction. He saw her instantly but continued puffing and panting his way towards her. She remained planted on the ground, staring at his swaying form. Just then, seconds before he reached her, his feet came to a sliding stop. They were yards from each other, each one searching the other for some kind of sign or signal. Then more forms began emerging from the gloom. The man glanced behind him and then, in a moment, he turned and ran off. An assembly of boots, uniforms and torch lights were now in view but instantly Nancy knew they would never reach him before he entered the woodland again. Without thinking she swung her body round and began running in the direction he had taken. Before long she could just make out the man's form. He was at the edge of the wood now, and his body dropped into a slower run as he began picking his way between the dense undergrowth. With her eyes fixed upon his figure, Nancy strained onwards reaching as fast a sprint as possible, so it was with great force that she was flung into the arms of another man coming towards her. She had not seen him, but suddenly her propulsion was broken and someone was reaching out his hands to stop her. She jolted and sprang back. It was only then that she saw the one who now held her shoulders with his outstretched arms. It was Peach.

"What the blazes are you doing?" he shouted at her.

"He's there, he's there!" Nancy began screaming and pointing into the woods. The assembly had by now reached her and Peach beckoned them.

"Get back to the van now!" he barked at her. He turned to join his men, leaving Nancy alone. She stood there, eyes blazing and heart pounding, all the time straining her eyes into the woodland. All she could see now was the frantic movement of the pursuing squad.

A hand suddenly gripped her arm and Nancy saw Miss Halsall beside her. "You heard him: let's get you back to the van, you idiot!" she shouted. Miss Halsall marched her back towards the van door, forced her inside before she climbed in herself and slammed the door shut behind them. She motioned for Nancy to sit down. A few moments later there was more shouting and gunshots. "You, stay here this time," shouted Miss Halsall just before she jumped out of the van again, shutting the door behind her.

It seemed a long time before anything else happened, but eventually someone banged on the van's back window, a signal to move on. Nancy was still alone, for no-one had returned. She had continued to listen to the movements and shouts of the men and women until they grew quieter. In truth, she had no idea what was happening outside. The van pulled away slowly. Out of the window Nancy saw the woodland disappear and felt the ride smooth out again. "We must be back on the road to town," she thought.

Then it happened! The blast was instant, its sound more enormous than anything Nancy had heard before, even that first night of the bombing. Instantly the van was forced onto its side. There was another blast, smaller this time, but closer. The darkness of the van had disappeared and a great light and heat now flooded the back. Nancy managed to lift herself on her arms before she twisted herself around and reached out for the door, yanking the handle. Thankfully, the door opened and she climbed out and began to run. Only when she reached the other side of the road did she look back. The scene was truly horrible. She was parallel to the railway track: ahead of her a goods train had been folded in two by an explosion. The front half of the train lay on its side in the clearing between the track and the road. Further back she could see flames spewing from the containers, their metal frames had already started to buckle in the flames and heat, making a kind of metallic yawning noise.

The shocked van driver and other people arrived quickly. They drew Nancy further back from the road and looked across towards the carnage in despair, shouting to each other in anger. Eventually, fire engines arrived and blankets were draped around Nancy as she was walked up the road to a waiting car. An arm appeared around Nancy's shoulder as she walked. Looking up, she saw it was young officer. He was shouting something at her about being "safe now" and "not to worry". He guided her into the car and she was soon driven away.

A MYSTERIOUS JOURNEY

2010

Arthur didn't ask Mr Smith about the reporter's visit, although he was very curious to know more. What did he mean 'he was more than that'; more than what? One day he noticed that Mr Smith seemed sad and distant. His jaw was clenched and his entire body, although so frail, was tense. After a while Arthur got up to go and Mr Smith looked up for the first time. "What do you do for the rest of the day, on a Saturday I mean?" he asked.

Arthur was surprised by the question. Never before had Mr Smith shown any interest in his life aside from his time at the house. "Depends," he said. "Sometimes I have to go to the shops with Mum. Sometimes I just ride around on my bike."

Mr Smith nodded and looked back down at his teacup. "What if I asked you to come somewhere with me?" he asked without looking up.

"Where?"

"Oh, not far; somewhere just out of town."

"Yeah, I suppose. I mean, if you want to."

"Would I have to ask your parents' permission?"

"I can ask them."

Mr Smith looked at him. "Good, good; it's not far, just on the edge of town. It's very public. Well, shall we say next Saturday then? We can go out in the morning, save you working in the garden as well."

"Yeah, yeah, I guess."

Mr Smith got up to see Arthur to the door. "Next week then," he said. "Next week."

The day arrived and Arthur was awake early. The house was quiet, so he slowly turned the key in the lock of the front door and slipped out. Arriving at Mr Smith's, the door opened before he had the chance to knock. Mr Smith was already up. "Right then," he said, with forced cheerfulness. "Of course it's a fool's errand, all this, but nothing like a trip out, eh?" Arthur had no idea what a 'fool's errand' was.

Mr Smith locked the door behind them and they set off for the bus stop: Arthur striding out in front, the man's slow, deliberate steps forcing him to lag behind. They came to The Green and stopped outside the post office. Mr Smith reached into his pocket for some mints and offered one up to his friend.

They caught the number 22 bus which took them towards the edge of the town. Mr Smith did not speak but simply sat upright, staring ahead.

The bus dropped them off beside an entrance to a housing estate. Large, expensive houses flanked the road and more swept away into the distance. Mr Smith pointed at them. "They're new," he said. "But I haven't been up here in more than fifty years so what does that tell you?"

The air was starting to feel thick from the summer sun and pollen from the crops growing in a nearby field.

"Where are we going?" Arthur asked.

"Now that's a good question," came the reply. "I told you I've not been here in many a year, and it's changed." Mr Smith looked left and right. "It was virtually all fields all those years ago," he said. He reached into his pocket, pulled out a handkerchief and wiped his forehead before he looked around again. There was a pub across the road and a garage next door. Mr Smith pointed. "I reckon it must be over there somewhere," he said. They began to walk across the road.

"Perhaps if you tell me what we're looking for I can help," said Arthur.

"A cemetery, boy," said the old man.

"A cemetery?" The only cemetery Arthur knew was in town.

"This is a special cemetery, lad."

By now they were on the other side of the road. Mr Smith stopped and looked around again. He looked confused, even disappointed. A young man was coming towards them on the pavement. He was jogging and looked very sweaty and red. Arthur stepped aside to let him past but Mr Smith put up his hand to get the man's attention. The runner stopped. "What's, up?" he said between gulps for air. "Can I help?"

"I hope so," said Mr Smith, "I'm looking for the War cemetery."

The runner put his hands on his hips and gulped some more. His chest was heaving in and out. "It's on the old Barrows Hill Road; this is the new Barrows Hill Road, well, built in the '70s if you call that new," he said between heavy breaths.

"You mean it's not here?"

"It's half a mile that way." The runner pointed to a road that sprouted out just beyond the garage. "That will take you down to it," he said.

Mr Smith thanked him and turned to Arthur. They linked arms and began shuffling towards the junction. It turned out to be a modern road with houses down both sides. It all reminded Arthur of his own street and his own home. At the bottom they came to a T-junction and Arthur saw a sign: 'Old Barrows Hill'. He helped Mr Smith across the road. There was a large triangle of grass, wide at first and then narrowing to a set of gates. In front there was a large sign, reading: 'Orethorpe Second World War Cemetery'.

"I've never been here before," said Arthur.

"I don't suppose many your age have. They had to build it, you know like a special one-off, so many were killed."

"When, when were they killed?"

"World War Two, that's when. Don't they teach you history at school?"

"I guess."

Beyond the gates was a wide driveway lined with tall trees. Nothing else could be seen from the road. Arthur waited for Mr Smith to move, but he just stood there, silent and still.

"Aren't we going in?" asked Arthur eventually.

But they didn't go in and, to his surprise, the old man turned his back. He stepped out into the road, but there was a cyclist coming and he had to stumble back to avoid her.

"Steady!" cried Arthur, springing forward to take his friend's hand. "Take it easy or you'll get hurt."

The old man took out his handkerchief once more. He wiped his hands and the back of his neck before putting it back in his pocket. He turned to Arthur. "I'm sorry, lad, this has all been a waste of time."

"Just tell me why we're here. Is it something to do with that reporter?"

"It was very wrong of me to bring you out here, Arthur, very wrong, I see that now," said Mr Smith, ignoring his question. "I've no right to pull you into this. I'm just a very old man with memories that have no place among the very young."

"What do you mean? What memories?"

"Ones that should be buried with the past, ones that deserve to be dead as I probably deserve to be."

They walked slowly back to the bus stop. Mr Smith wearily sat down on a plastic seat underneath the covering of the shelter. Arthur sat next to him. "At least tell me why you wanted to come," he asked.

"I've told you, memories."

"Can't you tell me what of?"

"Part of me was hoping I could, but today is clearly not the day." He turned to look Arthur in the face. "And you're too young to understand, I see that now."

The ride back was hot and boring. Arthur saw Mr Smith back home. Both were weary. Mr Smith opened the kitchen door onto a dusty, untidy yard where there was a kind of patio. They sat on some old chairs. Arthur could hear the kettle in the kitchen. It had boiled and clicked itself off. He was about to get up to make the tea when Mr Smith said something to him. "Look up there," he said, pointing to the sky. "What do you see?"

Arthur was puzzled. "Blue sky and a few clouds; why?"

"And at night?"

Arthur shrugged. "I don't know; the moon, stars."

"Well as they won't tell you, I will. They talk about a beautiful black sky, a silver moon and the star dust of the Milky Way. Paah, shall I tell you what I see at night? I see the expanse of space as an electronic spinal cord carrying thousands, if not millions, of unseen messages from person to person." He craned his head further back. "The sky isn't an unspoilt and unpolluted space and hasn't been for many years. It's an unseen sphere crammed with the human junk of suspicion and betrayal."

AFTERMATH

1940

Nancy awoke in a strange bed. She looked around the room. It was small, with exposed, painted brickwork reaching up to a high ceiling with pipes across it. There was a single bed, a plain cabinet of dark wood and a matching desk. A small, thin rug provided the only colour.

It was the morning after the blast and the images of that terrible event immediately flashed into her mind. She reached out to touch her cheek to check if the heat of the flames had left a mark. She had been pushed into a car and driven back to Megg House. After a long time she had been told that the railway line had been bombed, a train derailed and at least three people killed. The spies were responsible. She knew it, and so did everyone else at Megg House, and, as she would soon learn, everyone in Orethorpe itself. The spies had attacked the railway line to stop the delivery of bombs and munitions from the town's factories. They had also done it to terrify everyone, weaken their spirit. Later she also overheard that they had failed to capture the man at Graves End Wood. Somehow he had managed to slide and duck and scoop his way over, through and between the bracken, tree roots and branches of the woodland to a place of obscurity.

Back at Megg House the previous night she had frantically tried to find Peach to tell him the identity of the man, but he was nowhere to be seen. Eventually Sir had appeared with several men and had come over. She had gabbled out what she knew.

"And you're sure it's him?" he had said when she had finished.

"I'm absolutely certain."

He had put his arm around her and signalled for her to be given a bed for the night. She was led down to the basement, along one of the corridors leading away from Number 10, which she now knew was officially called the Map Room, into a bedroom, and immediately fell into an exhausted sleep.

Waking she noticed her clothes scattered over the chair beside the desk. She dressed quickly. The corridor outside was empty, but as Nancy walked towards Number 10 she heard voices. Opening the door she saw Sir standing in the centre of the lower level. The morning briefing was already in full swing.

"Of course, we knew it was coming and now it's here," said Sir. "The town is understandably terrified and that makes containing our job here harder, but it could also help," he continued. "There are far too many of them out there for us to watch alone."

"We need more men," someone shouted from across the room.

"And we may just get them," he replied. "It's not just a threat anymore, it's real; they're real and they're active."

The briefing inside Number 10 went on for some time. Eventually Nancy felt a tugging on her arm. It was

Miss Halsall. "Sir says you're not to disappear; he needs to speak to you," she said, her voice soft. "Tell you what, let's start with some breakfast while we're waiting, shall we?"

The pair walked out of Number 10 and down another corridor Nancy hadn't seen before. Room after room sprouted off it. Most of the doors were closed, but sometimes Nancy would catch a glance of a sparse room with a small, thinly made bed and a worn-looking wooden desk. In another room she saw a row of uniformed women seated behind desks and typewriters. As they turned a sharp left and into another corridor, Nancy could hear animated voices talking to each other. Miss Halsall continued to march down the corridor in military fashion but, on passing a door, Nancy looked inside the room to see a group of middle-aged men sat around a long, polished table. Papers and maps had been placed in the middle of the table and some of the men were on their feet, leaning over the documents. Several were speaking at once. She would have liked to have seen more but an unseen hand suddenly swung the door shut from the inside.

There was another staircase, equally narrow to the one she knew. A sign read, 'Way Out to Intercept Room'. Opposite it were two double doors, both open, leading to a canteen Nancy had never seen before. It was small and the tables so tightly packed together that they almost formed one long, continuous row. Miss Halsall went up to the counter and ordered tea and toast for them both. "Sorry about all this hanging around," she said, placing a tin mug in front of Nancy.

"That's all right," said Nancy. "It's been a rough night for us all."

"Especially us, you and me I mean. What a mess. Sir's in trouble if we don't make progress soon."

Miss Halsall lifted her mug to her lips and took a loud gulp. "Come to think of it, we're all in trouble if we don't get a breakthrough, and fast." She took several more gulps of her tea and motioned that they hadn't much time.

The door to the small canteen opened. Nancy got a start when she saw Peach walk up to the counter. She hadn't seen or spoken to him since the night before. She watched as he took a small mug over to a table against a wall and slumped down. He looked exhausted. His hair was uncombed, his uniform splattered with mud. What's more, his face was drawn and grey. He glanced over towards them and merely nodded at Miss Halsall before casting his eyes down again.

"Been a bad, bad night," said Miss Halsall, taking another large gulp of her drink.

After breakfast they went back into Number 10. Sir was standing on the upper level, talking to a uniformed man seated behind one of the desks. To Nancy's surprise Sir smiled as he turned to her. "What did I tell you about finding yourself in the centre of things, eh?" he said. "Now you've gone and done it again: not that I'm complaining."

"Have you found the man yet?" she asked, her voice eager.

"No, but we've been over to the teacher's house and will do so again now. I want you to go along and say if you recognise anyone else in the house, if you recognise the man among the other tenants."

"But Miss Temple knows who I am."

"That's easy to explain: we'll just say you saw someone suspicious running through town last night and reported it. Come on."

They rounded one of the corners of the long corridor in the basement and almost bumped into Peach coming the other way.

"Where on earth have you been?" shouted Sir.

Peach stiffened his back and saluted. "Just trying to clear things up, Sir."

"You missed the briefing, man, that's inexcusable."

"Yes, Sir, I'm sorry."

"Where on earth have you been all night? No-one has seen you?"

"Like I said, here and there trying to sort things out, Sir, I'm sorry you missed me."

"I'll have to brief you myself. My office in ten."

"Yes, Sir," said Peach, his voice weak.

Half an hour later Nancy and Peach made their way into town. Peach drove in silence. The car came to a stop outside a row of neat, pretty houses with bay windows and small front lawns. "Best I go in alone," said Peach.

"But Sir said."

"Never mind what Sir said, he's obviously not thinking straight," said Peach, interrupting her. "If last night taught us anything it's that they are deadly serious and they wouldn't think twice about picking off a girl like you."

Nancy watched as he left the car and drew his coat further around his weary frame. He walked up to one of the heavy front doors and knocked. The door was opened by a young woman: not Miss Temple, but about the same age. The door closed behind them.

It was more than an hour before the door opened again. Nancy was jolted by the sight of Miss Temple at the door this time. Nancy shrunk down in her seat, trying to hide herself from view. But she need not have worried as the door was quickly shut again. Peach jumped into the car and started the engine.

"That was her, Miss Temple, my schoolteacher, the one in the café," said Nancy.

"I know," replied Peach.

"Well, what did she say?"

Peach began to pull the car away. "She said she doesn't hardly knows the man and doesn't know where he's living; besides, her whereabouts last night can be confirmed by others, she told me. She says he doesn't even work in the town. He told her he was a teacher working miles away on a visit to a friend in Orethorpe."

"And you believe her?"

"Well the other lodgers there vouched for her and I'm told there are others to back up her story. She met him in the café for the first time and they got talking, that's all."

"But shouldn't you arrest her, to be sure?" Nancy was beginning to feel angry at his lack of interest and apparent reluctance to act. This was the best lead they'd had, wasn't it? What was wrong with him?

But he didn't reply. He simply looked ahead, the hounded look of last night sweeping over his features again. Nancy's anger grew.

"Look," she said, swinging around in her seat, "you have to do something more about this. She could get away and then what?"

"Arrest her, eh? On what grounds?"

"She was with him, she was talking to him." Nancy was almost shouting now.

Peach shouted back. "And she says she hardly knows him."

They came to a stop at a junction. "Now listen," said Peach, his voice calm. "The town is full of fear with everyone looking for a spy under every stone. If I arrest her now it will be the gossip of every drawing room before evening. And I can't afford to tip him off if she really doesn't know him well. If that's true then there's a chance he doesn't know we have someone who can identify him." He glanced over towards Nancy. "So, for now, we will have this street watched, if that meets with your approval?"

Nancy said nothing. They drove along in silence for several minutes before Peach spoke again. "Sir says you're to stay at Megg House for a further few days, overnight I mean," he said. "He's arranging for a message to be sent to your parents so your cover story is, well, covered, if you see what I mean. I would ask if that is agreeable to you but it's actually an order."

"Fine with me," said Nancy as she watched the houses pass by.

WORKING AT MEGG HOUSE

1940

Over the next few days Nancy saw little beyond Number 10 and none of the town beyond the gardens of Megg House. It wasn't long before she was given extra work. Over the coming days she acted as an unofficial 'runner' between Number 10 and the rooms and huts above ground.

She would start her day in the Intercept Room. There she would be handed the intercepts of the past twelve hours, along with notes made by the Commanding Officer of that night's shift. From there she would make her way to the Filter Room where, she'd learned, the intercepts were read and sorted. Those considered especially interesting or potentially important were singled out for Number 10. Finally, she would make her way to Number 10.

"And don't forget the milk 'cos they can't contemplate the thought of black tea," Miss Halsall had told her. Every morning at 8 o'clock sharp, two fresh bottles of milk would be placed at the top of the stairs leading down to Number 10. It became Nancy's job to take it down, as it would be a Wren's when further deliveries were made at 2 o'clock and 7 o'clock.

Once inside Number 10, Nancy would deposit the documents and daily reports into a tray on the desk next to the large map in the middle of the room. She now noticed, for the first time, that the map also highlighted the locations of vulnerable targets such as the factories, the railway lines and the coal stores and, additionally, where the authorities were based, including the police and air raid wardens. "That way if we need to move fast we alert those people up there," a Wren had told Nancy, pointing up towards the row of chairs on the upper deck.

Nancy knew that anything really revealing would be telephoned directly to Number 10 from the ground above, but she still liked the sensation of trust and responsibility given to her. She had begun to feel a part of the tightly-woven, intricate fabric of Megg House.

Her arrival in Number 10 coincided with the beginning of the morning meeting. Sir was usually already there, and within a few minutes the room was packed with uniforms gathered around the central map. This was the handover meeting, the time when the night and day shifts overlapped, and a chance to reflect on the success or failure of the past twenty-four hours. Were the spies transmitting? If so, how many and for how long? What was the frequency? When were they intercepted? What did they mean? What about direction finding, can it give us an area? What intelligence was there from around the town? What were the police or the Home Guard picking up? Had anyone seen an abandoned car, heard a suspicious-sounding accent or a thread of gossip? It was the night duty officer's job to answer all these questions.

One particular morning Sir had, as usual, listened to the briefing in relative silence. Then he retrieved a folder from under his arm and said in a grave and deeply serious voice: "Public awareness has been, rather predictably, heightened after the bombing. The fear out there is getting worse. I know many of you are exhausted but what happened has made this work more crucial than ever. Keep at it and we WILL get the breakthrough we need. We WILL defeat them and we WILL win this War."

Nancy carried out several 'postal' and 'delivery' rounds between the ground floor rooms inside the house, the huts scattered across the lawns and Number 10 each day. She had stopped going to the canteen across the lawn for lunch, preferring the small one near Number 10.

When 4 o'clock came around she would spring up the steps of Number 10 for the last time and head for the Intercept Room. There she would carry out her intercepts. The noise from the other wireless sets and interceptors sometimes made it harder to pick out Morse code from the usual interference on the wires. Several times she had had to call over the supervisor to confess to missing a letter or two.

"We're all in the same boat, love, but do what you can," the supervisor had said to her. "That's all we can do: the best we can."

Nancy had become one of those who ate, slept and spent much of their day and night in a windowless, subterranean warren. And so it was that she spent more than a week at Megg House while barely noticing the world outside. One morning, after breakfast, she finally emerged from Megg House to return home. Walking down the hill towards the town centre, she had been amazed by the sight of a heavy white frost on the pavements and roads. "Perhaps we are in for a long, hard winter," she thought to herself.

She got another surprise when she opened the front door to the house; Father was home. She saw his feet and hands poking from around the armchair in front of the fire. Going up to him, she smiled cheerily. "Hello Dad, you okay?"

He looked up at her gravely but said nothing.

"What's up, what's happened?" said Nancy, feeling suddenly alarmed.

"There's been a bombing in town, love. You'd better sit down. Mother will be back soon and she can tell you more."

"You mean the Germans?"

"Well, sort of, but not in the way you know."

Just then Nancy heard the front door open and then slam shut. Mother came bustling through into the room. "Goodness me, have you been travelling through the night?" she said, removing her headscarf.

Nancy knew that her parents had been told she was away on a special course. "No," she said. Anxious to change the subject she added: "Dad's saying we've been bombed again."

Mother placed her shopping bag on the table with a loud thud. She began to take off her gloves. "Everyone's terrified, that's what. The railway track was bombed a week ago, on the very day you left. Would've been frantic had we not been told you'd gone by bus. Where've you been anyway?"

"If you mean about the railway line being bombed then I already know. They told us when we were on the course." Nancy wanted to keep the conversation away from herself.

"They reckon the Germans did it," said Father.

"Of course they did it: who else would want to blow up a track carrying goods from the factory?" said Mother. "It's a right nasty business. You can't walk from here to town and back without being stopped a dozen times. Everyone's after the latest gossip."

"They're scared, love," said Father, staring gravely into the fire.

"Everyone looks at each other funny," said Mother. "I was stood talking with Mrs Smith and her daughter when this man, really smartly dressed, sauntered past, whistling with his hands in his pockets. Not a factory worker, that's for sure, too smart for that. We just looked at each other wondering if he's a spy."

"Maybe he was simply taking a girl to the pictures," said Father. He heaved himself up out of the chair with a deep sigh. He walked into the kitchen and moments later Nancy heard the back door opening and then close.

"Maybe, and maybe he's one of those Germans come to smash us all to kingdom come," said Mother under her breath.

SNOOPING

2010

After their trip to the cemetery, Arthur and Mr Smith didn't see each other for a fortnight as Arthur was in Cornwall with his family on a camping holiday. At night, sitting outside the tent, he would look up into the sky and remember Mr Smith's strange words about betrayal and the night sky carrying strange messages. Arthur didn't know any old people apart from his grandparents but they hadn't much of a clue about the internet or satellites or that kind of thing, so how could Mr Smith?

One day he was in a little gift shop when he saw a poster with a War slogan on it. "Keep Calm and Carry On" it said. Arthur had bought it for his friend, thinking he might like to have a cheery slogan from the War. But approaching Mr Smith's house on the first Saturday after returning home he found he was nervous about seeing him again.

Mr Smith opened the door and smiled as usual. Arthur held out the poster. It was curled into a roll. "I brought you something," he said.

"Oh, how kind, you shouldn't have," said Mr Smith, taking it from him.

They went into the kitchen where Mr Smith unfurled his gift on the table. Arthur was relieved to see him chuckle a little.

"Very good, very good," he said, smiling.

"You really like it?"

"Oh yes. And we did, you know, we did carry on: well, we had no choice you see."

"Is that why we went to the cemetery the other week?" The words were out before Arthur could stop them.

Mr Smith looked at him. "Never mind that: it shouldn't have happened and I apologise," he said. "I should keep the past where it is and leave the young to their innocence. It won't happen again."

Arthur did some tidying in the front garden while his friend prepared refreshments of tea and scones. The small border closest to the house ran underneath a window on the opposite side of the door to the living room. It too had a small bay window, and Arthur had always presumed it to be Mr Smith's bedroom. After some particularly heavy weeding he pulled himself up to have a stretch and found himself glancing into the room. The curtains had been half drawn, but through the gap Arthur could see boxes. They were piled up, one on top of the other, and next to them were some filing cabinets.

Later, while he and Mr Smith sat in the kitchen, the old man made a surprise announcement. "I've got to go out in a bit, but you've almost finished, haven't you?"

Arthur thought quickly. "Well, almost, but I want to do a bit more."

"Well don't overdo it, it's still quite hot. The summer is lingering this year."

Arthur's mind turned over. He wanted to get into that room, just to have a look, just to glance over the cabinets and boxes to see if they might hold the clues to his friend's secrets. "I won't open anything," he told himself.

"Will you leave the front door open so I can use the toilet?" he asked.

"Yes, but make sure you close it firmly when you leave."

Not long afterwards Mr Smith climbed onto his mobility scooter and waved him goodbye. "The door is on the latch but remember what I said," he called out as the tiny engine whirled down the path.

It was at least ten minutes before Arthur felt it was safe to put down his trowel and go back inside. The door to the mysterious room was shut. As Arthur reached out to touch the handle he felt a sharp stab of guilt but his curiosity was stronger. The door opened easily and he went inside. Looking around he counted twelve boxes arranged into four columns around the walls. Beside them were several tall filing cabinets. All were wooden and all looked old.

The air in the room was still and silent and Arthur could hear his own breath. Once more he began to feel ashamed. "I said I won't open anything and I won't," he said to himself.

He took another look round, but there was nothing new, previously unnoticed, to give him any more clues. He turned to leave, but as he did so he did see something else. Beside the wall, close to the door, there was a very old-looking case. He bent down to look at it. It was large and black with many scratches over the leather surface. Two rusty clasps held it together. He reached over and grabbed hold of the leather strap to pull it closer, but was yanked back. It was too heavy, way too heavy for him to even move. He was certain he could not lift it. He looked again and saw something else. Behind the case, wedged between the wall and the back of one of the cabinets, there was something smaller. It was a briefcase. This he *could* move, and he successfully pulled it away. He placed it upon the carpet in front of him.

It was brown and looked every bit as old as the other furniture in the room. Arthur crouched down to see closer. The colour was patchy and the leather creased. It too had a rusty clasp. He pulled it towards him. It was light and felt empty. He pulled it open. He was right: it was empty, or at least it appeared so at first. Then he saw the outline of something in the top fold. He reached in. His hand clasped around something and he pulled it out. It was three photographs. The paper itself was buckled like it had been held underwater. Holding them up to the light, Arthur could see they were faded, but the images could still be clearly seen. The first was of two young boys, no older than ten. Both were wearing sailor outfits and were standing against a dark background. One was seated, the other standing by his side. Arthur put the photograph down and picked up the second. This was larger, with more people. It was a family group of around ten people. An old woman, draped in black, was seated in the centre. Her hair had been pulled tightly back and she wore a white broach at her throat. Surrounding her were figures of varying ages, the women in long, dark skirts and high-necked blouses, the men wearing suits and hats. A baby was seated on a young woman's knee, and another, older child was seated on the floor amongst the folds of her skirt. All stared out at Arthur with unsmiling mouths and serious eyes.

Arthur flipped the photograph over. Several words had been printed on the back.

Gacek
Studio fotograficzne Dunajski
Warszawa
1889

He picked up the first one again and flipped that over, but it was blank. The third photograph was of a young man in uniform standing proudly against a background of trees. He wore a uniform and a cap, and clutched beside him a huge rifle. At the bottom, in tiny print, was the name.

RANK Albert Schmitt, 1918

Arthur got up and went into the kitchen where he found a chewed pen and a scrap of paper. He went back into the room and crouched down to copy the words. Afterwards he returned the photographs and propped the briefcase back against the wall. He put the paper in his pocket and went outside, closing the front door firmly behind him.

SNOW

1940

The snow arrived. Every day the leaden clouds would form over the hills and fields of Orethorpe before the wind carried them into town.

In winters past Nancy would skip and jump about in the fluffy mess and delight in the red, green and gold of Christmas lights and wrappings crammed in the shops of Orethorpe. She had loved the taste and smell of winter then, and had not taken a single memory of being cold and unhappy into her almost-teenage years. But since the War she had begun to hate the cold rooms, the biting air and, now, the seemingly constant snow on snow. Her daily walk to school was taking twice as long as she slid along the ice-packed pavements which were now unrecognisable from the roads themselves. Once she saw a bus slide across the road towards Simpsons, the chemist shop, before it was stopped by a great mound of snow piled up against the arched window. The factories added their own flavour to the innocent, white covering over the town, for the frantic pace of construction was sending more and more black smoke into the air. It stuck to the white mounds, turning a soft icing into the colour of death.

It was not long before Orethorpe began to run out of coal. The factories' constant and inexhaustible demand for fuel had been understood in the beginning, but, as the weather changed for the worse, so did the minds of many. They spoke constantly of the rapidly dwindling supplies. One night Father had come in through the back door from the yard and informed his wife and youngest child that they were only to light a fire in the evenings if they could possibly manage and were to be out much of the day. A week later Nancy took home a letter stating that the school would be going down to half days until supplies could be restored.

But the people of Orethorpe were not beaten so easily and, as usual, the town hall was open for afternoon tea, dances and evening events. Joyce's mother had popped in one afternoon between these excitements to enthuse to Mother and whoever would listen.

"Sooo lovely to be safely on your feet again, Margaret, without fear of them giving way beneath you, like out there," she jabbed her finger towards the window. "Oh why don't you consent to come with us to the next dance? My James would jump at the chance of having another gorgeous lady to carry around the floor."

"Ernie and Audrey are working all hours as you know," said Mother. "They keep altering the shifts and I swear they sometimes run over so much that they've scarce finished one when t'other is about to begin."

Nancy had often thought it odd that her own mother, with no sons on active service to really fret about, had found it so hard to adapt to the hardships of the War, while Mrs Harris, with a boy in uniform and another about to join him, carried such an air of cheerfulness, even if it did, at times, resemble a flashy ribbon around something excessively plain.

Nancy was no longer sleeping at Megg House after her shifts but she sensed that the time was coming when she would be living there again. The chaos that accompanied the bombing had required her full-time attention, and now it had been replaced by a new, quiet tension.

One day everyone in the Intercept Room was being briefed by Sir. "Your intercepts won't be in German Morse anymore," he said. "The spies have switched to using encrypted codes so you won't understand them when they come through."

There was silence. "What it means is this," he continued. "We intercept thousands of German Morse messages everyday. It's no longer simply a question of German being put into Morse code. No, now they're encrypted, most of them, using some ingenious device called the Enigma machine. We haven't a clue what they say, but we pass them on to people who might be able to find out, who might be able to make sense of them one day. Anyway, even if we can't read them and understand them we can still trace the signal used to transmit them on. That, for now, is our best hope."

Shortly after his announcement Sir asked her to take on extra shifts. "The vans are out all night, every night, we're that desperate," Sir had told her. "Can we put you down for some more shifts?"

"Yes, if I can come up with a reasonable excuse," said Nancy. "Mum and Dad didn't suspect last time, thankfully, but everyone is suspicious about this place."

"You have to trust me on this: arrangements will be made," he said.

He was true to his word, and soon it seemed to Nancy that she spent much of her waking time sat on a hard chair in the Intercept Room crouched over a large, hot radio receiver. Most of the time she heard nothing. The spies were not stupid and only transmitted when they absolutely had to. But on a handful of occasions she flew into an exchange like a Spitfire straying into a dogfight over the English Channel. Before Sir's announcement she had begun to notice something about them: they were always on the same frequency and they always began with the same long, continuous tone followed by three quick taps of the Morse code, producing three 'bips' as she liked to call them. The operator, whoever he was, appeared quite jumpy, and they would sometimes stop abruptly and then appear to go back to the beginning to repeat the message again. It was as if they were new to radio work, new perhaps to spying. Even after the messages had turned to codes, Nancy noticed the same pattern. Somehow, she began to form an imaginary picture of the person at the other end of the faint dits and dots. They could be in the nearby town having caught a bus or a train there, wanting to put distance between themselves and Megg House. Or, they could be in the next field beyond the house's grounds. The spy could be crouched over a spy set in a remote, rural location or sitting down in a dingy bedroom in one of the many terraced houses in the town. He could have smiled at his landlady this morning, eaten breakfast with the other lodgers and, only afterwards, excused himself to go up to his own room. There he could have waited for silence until he pulled the set, disguised as a suitcase, out from underneath his bed and carefully unfurled the wires. He would open the door of his room to make sure that no-one was listening before he would sit down on the bedroom floor and tap out his vital message. The name of the game was not to get caught but, really, there would be only one real aim: the town's ultimate destruction.

LEAFLETS

1940

Nancy was longing to spend more and more time within the secret confines of Megg House and its grounds. Beyond its lawns and huts was a town in the grip of spy-mania. The prospect of spies, even their very presence inside the town, had turned from a half-whispered fear into a full-blown obsession. Sir's first reaction had been to say nothing, but the fear and suspicion had grown so fast and the progress of the House was so slow that one day he suddenly announced a change of direction.

"We need help and we need it fast," he had told the assembled group during one morning briefing. "We're up here but the real intelligence could be out there, and we need help gathering it in." Posters and leaflets had been produced by the War Office, he said, and these were to be distributed throughout the town. While they would stop short of admitting the presence of an actual spy ring, the public would be urged to look out for and report any suspicious talk or activity.

After the briefing had finished Peach approached Nancy. "We need help giving them out: you willing and able?" he asked.

"Sure, as always," she had replied.

He drove them into town, parked up and got out to open the boot. Several boxes were stacked inside. He reached in and pulled out a wad of leaflets. "Just start pushing them through doors," he said.

Nancy glanced down at one of the leaflets. A coloured pencil drawing showed a woman in the foreground. Her hand was resting on her chin and her head was cocked towards the mysterious, shadowy figure beside her. 'DON'T HELP THE ENEMY WITHIN' read the heading. Underneath the picture were several instructions on how to detect or spot a potential spy. 'Do they use English words not in common use? Do they have trouble handling English money? Do they make silly mistakes over place names or famous people? Do they keep irregular hours'? At the bottom read the bold words, 'IF **YOU** LOOK OUT WE WON'T GET CAUGHT OUT.

After several minutes they approached a house with thick net curtains on the inside of the front door. The letterbox was stiff and made a loud snapping sound as it sprung back.

"And what does this tell us about the immediate spy threat?" Nancy heard a young voice as the door opened. A young couple, a man and a woman, emerged. Both were smartly dressed, him in a grey suit and overcoat, she in a pencil skirt, jacket with fur trim and a smart hat from which protruded a tall feather. The man was holding the leaflet.

"It says nothing about any direct threat, only that everyone has to keep a watch out," replied Peach.

"But it's clearly more than that," said the man. "Everywhere you go people are talking about it. You can't tell me it's not suspected here. What about that train?"

Peach's face remained blank. "Asking people to be vigilant is our responsibility, as is protecting life where we can. It's the responsibility of folks like yourselves to help us in the task."

"As you want to remind us," said the man, holding the leaflet up to make his point.

"Exactly," replied Peach.

"May I give you some advice, as a member of the public," said the man. "You need to start telling your public more, otherwise wild rumours start. Like I said, the railway accident, the fatal one, you wouldn't believe some of the theories going around about that."

"And what about that place at the top of the hill?" the woman interjected

"What about it?"

"Well, there are rumours about that place too," she said. "It's all very mysterious, you have to admit. Do you work there?"

To Nancy's surprise Peach let out a snort of laughter. "You do underestimate us if you think we can talk about anything and everything. You know what it's like in War. We, all of us, are informed on a need-to-know basis, however dull the truth actually is."

"But you're missing my point," the man retorted again. "By saying so little you're creating fertile ground for rumour and greater fear. Why not open the window on your operations and allow a little more light in, eh?"

"These are decisions for those more senior than me; now, will you excuse me? We have work to do," said Peach.

Nancy watched the couple close their door and walk away.

"You can't blame them, I suppose," she said.

"Yes you can," said Peach. "It's sheer nosiness and wanting to know more than everyone else, nothing more."

"But they're right: everyone is afraid," said Nancy. "First they were afraid of the bombings, now they're afraid of virtually everyone they see in the street."

Peach studied her for several moments. "And you believe we're losing this, don't you?" he challenged.

"I didn't say that."

"Why not? You'd be right. We're intercepting messages we can't understand and chasing the shadow of faint dots and dashes across a map."

Nancy noticed he looked thinner than usual. Great dark bags had appeared under his eyes. Since the explosion on the railway track he had lost his carefree grin and easy manner. Now he was greyer, more solemn and, thought Nancy, rather afraid.

"What about that man I saw in the woods and Miss Temple, why haven't those clues led us to them?" she asked.

He took her elbow and leant down to whisper. "Talk about careless talk," he scolded. "I told you, the man pushed off that night and no-one else there knows anything."

"So you're not even watching to see if he comes back?"

Peach's grip on her arm grew tighter. He leant in further.

"In case you haven't noticed, we don't have a thousand men. We're doing what we can but don't you go repeating anything about that to anyone, you understand?"

Nancy struggled away from his grip. "Fine," she said.

He stepped back and walked over to the car, popping the boot open. Without speaking he reached in to pull out more leaflets, dropped the boot door and made for another street, handing Nancy another bundle as he passed by.

It was hours before Peach suggested they stop for the day. "Didn't realise the time; I've got to get back: you want a lift home?" he asked.

"No, no: I'll walk, thanks." His earlier tone had irritated her and she did not want to hear any more of his talk about how they were losing the search for the spies.

The walk took her past the street Nancy had visited with the Guides the day after it had been bombed. Further up the hill was a row of more expensive houses, including the house she had visited with Peach, the one where Miss Temple lodged. She climbed the steady incline of the hill. Everything looked just the same as before. Just then a car pulled up outside the house. The large, black bonnet curved towards her view. A man was getting out. He was wearing a large, heavy-looking coat and a hat which covered his face from where Nancy was standing. But as he stretched himself out and turned to close the car door she was almost rocked backwards. It was Peach. She continued staring as he glanced briefly around him before he jogged up to the front door of the house and knocked. He only had to wait a few moments before the door swung open and

Miss Temple stood on the other side. Nancy saw Miss Temple's mouth move and Peach's head nod. A few moments later she stepped aside to allow him into the house before the door swiftly shut behind them.

Suddenly afraid of being discovered, Nancy swung her head around, looking for cover. There was a brightly-decorated shop on the corner. The door made a tingling sound as she pushed it open and a bald man was standing behind the counter. He smiled at her. Nancy smiled back, but then turned her back and walked the length of the front window. The window was large but the view out of it was partially blocked by posters. The bell above the door rang again and a young mother and a boy walked in. The boy wandered over to where she was and began picking up some tins that had been displayed in the window. Glancing up, Nancy saw that her line of sight out of the window now gave her a view down the street towards the house. The house looked just the same as before.

"What are you looking at?" said the young voice.

Nancy became aware of someone tugging at her coat. She looked down. The boy was staring up at her.

"What are you doing?" he asked, his eyes gazing upward behind his grey cap.

"Nothing; just watching to see if it snows," replied Nancy.

The shopkeeper and young mother had stopped talking and were also looking over towards her.

"Can I help you, Miss?" asked the shopkeeper. There was a tone of suspicion in his voice.

"No thank you, I was just checking it wasn't snowing," said Nancy, cheerfully.

She looked back and immediately got another shock. The door had opened again, and a moment later Peach and Miss Temple were on the path and walking towards the car. Peach opened the door for Miss Temple and she got inside. Peach walked around to the driver's door and a moment later the car was pulling away from the house.

THE ARREST

1940

As Nancy left the shop her mind was racing with thoughts of how she could alert Megg House. She had walked no more than five minutes when the air raid siren suddenly started. Nancy ran all the way home, managing to reach the family's shelter in the yard before the first blasts could be heard over one of the distant hills.

The raid lasted an hour. Afterwards, alone in her bedroom, Nancy paced about, playing out what had happened in her mind. She went back to the window and looked down the street. A car had pulled up on the pavement opposite. Three men, all dressed in black, emerged. There was a hard rattle on the front door, followed by voices, men's voices, in the front room. Nancy opened her bedroom door to listen. Mother's voice could be heard over the men's now.

"You're taking him nowhere, do ya hear, what's he ever done?"

"I'm sorry, madam, but my orders are clear. Mr Brown is coming to answer a few questions, that's all. Nothing to be alarmed about, I'm sure."

"We need him here. He's the only man in the house."

"Well with any luck we'll soon sort this out and get it all cleared up in time for breakfast," came the reply.

"Breakfast! You're not questioning my husband all night! What's this about? I demand to know!"

By now Nancy was half-way down the stairs. Opening the door to the living room she saw the three men with their backs to her. Facing them were the wide-eyed faces of Mother, Father and Mary. Her father looked over to her. "It's all right lass; have we disturbed you? Go back upstairs, there's a good 'un," he said.

"What's going on?" asked Nancy.

"Someone's given the order for your father to be arrested," said Mother, her voice high-pitched with strain. "I reckon it's one of them no-good gossips down the town hall who want to know about his radio sets; well, they'll be sorry when I get hold of them: they'll…"

"Margaret, be quiet!" Nancy rarely heard her father raise his voice, least of all to her mother. It seemed almost unnatural coming from such a mild man. The three women of the household all gave a start.

Father turned back to Nancy. "It's just a misunderstanding, love. You know what it's like, everyone looking for a spy under every bush." He tried to snort a laugh, but it seemed to get stuck somewhere in his nose.

There was silence. The men didn't seem anxious to exert their authority and take control of the situation. Finally, Father himself broke the spell. "I suppose you want me in handcuffs then, officer?" he said.

"No need for that, Mr Brown, if you just come with us and we'll get this sorted out."

The men moved towards Father until they were either side of him. All four began to move for the door into the front room.

"Where are you taking him?" asked Mary.

"I can't tell you that Miss, but don't you worry; he'll be taken care of."

Nancy and Mary followed the men into the front room and watched as Father opened the front door and led the small group out, as if they were a band of friends on a fishing trip. When they returned to the living room Mother was slumped in a chair, a handkerchief to her cheek. "Why are they taking him? It's those, those *women*," she spat out the word.

Mother began to weep loudly, and soon Nancy noticed that the red, angry colour in her cheeks had drained to a white pallor. She remained slumped back into the chair. Several more minutes passed. Finally Mother broke the silence. "Where do you think they've taken him?" she asked.

"I don't know, police station I guess," replied Mary.

Mother began to weep again. "It's because of all those radios in the shed; I know it is, I know it is," she said, rocking herself backwards and forwards.

Mother refused to go to bed but, after some time, fell asleep in the chair. Eventually the sluggish dawn of winter broke. Mary crept out of the house, whispering to Nancy that she was going to the police station.

Nancy knew that the night wardens would be going home. Soon the factory workers would be snaking their way through the avenues and streets to start their early, half-day weekend shifts. She was worried about Father, desperately worried, but she also knew that she had to get up to Megg House to tell them what she had seen. She hadn't bothered to get undressed and it was simple to creep past Mother without waking her. She pulled on her coat and made for the front door.

A deep frost had formed into white crystals on the pavements and she found herself walking headlong into the bitter winter wind. It didn't take her long to reach the hill. She began to climb, noticing that here a winter mist had enveloped the higher ground. She could barely see more than a few yards in front of her, but she pressed on, her shoulders hunched and her hands in her pockets. She heard voices and dropped her head again and continued to climb. Then the voices came again. They were in front of her. Suddenly, out of the mist emerged two distinct figures. Within moments she was face-to-face with the tired forms of Father and Mary.

"Good grief, what are you doing here?" cried Mary.

For one moment all thoughts of Megg House were pushed aside and Nancy flung herself into her father's arms. "Are you all right, are you all right, what did they say?" she asked him.

He smiled down at her, but she could see that the skin around his eyes was dark with exhaustion and his brow was creased into deep wrinkles. "Oh fine, fine," he said in a cheery tone. "Like I told you last night, it's just a little mix-up. All's well now." He turned his head towards Mary in a gesture of reassurance. But she didn't smile.

"Did Mother send you, then?" asked Mary.

"No. I mean, not exactly. She's asleep. She...." Nancy trailed off. She reached up and hugged her father again.

"She'll be frantic if she finds you gone out the house as well," said Father in a light chuckle. He pulled her arms away from his neck, but took her right hand in his. Together, and without another word, the three of them descended the hill.

Back home Mother bustled around Father like an eighteen-year-old bride on her honeymoon. He had to sit in an easy chair by the fire, he must put his feet up, she insisted on him having the last egg for breakfast. Mary was ordered to light the fire; Nancy, to fetch the warm blanket from her parents' bed. Once the chill had been warmed from his frame and his skeleton relaxed, Father accepted the attention with ease and a little amusement. Occasionally he would glance up from his mug or plate and give Nancy a little wink.

No-one in the family questioned her about her solitary walk at dawn. All three had assumed she was on her way to the police station. But she knew she had to get away from home and up to Megg House, and soon. So, after breakfast, when Father and Mother were safely in the living room, she crept out of the house for the second time that day.

PEACH'S OFFICE

1940

Nancy sat in the Number 10 canteen, the one below ground. She stared into the mug wrapped around her small fingers. Suddenly the napkin stand in front of her began to move. It slid across the table, and as she looked up she saw Tom holding a wooden plotting stick. She had not heard him sit down.

"Where have you been?" she asked.

"I've had things to do; what's up?"

"I saw something, something so big I don't know what to do," she whispered.

Tom scrambled across several chairs until he was seated across from her. He leant in towards her. "Saw what exactly, you mean a spy?"

"I went to the house, the schoolteacher's house, the one with that man in the café," said Nancy. "I saw someone, someone we know going in." She moved towards him, their noses almost touching. "It was Peach."

She drew back, allowing the news to sink in. He too sat back in his chair, looking shocked.

"We have to know why he was there," said Nancy. "He's not been the same since that night in the wood when the railway line was also bombed and now…"

"So what? It doesn't necessarily mean anything." Tom was looking at her.

"It means he knows her and that he's involved more than we know." She hissed at him.

He leant in to her again. "Or maybe he's just doing his job and watching and, I don't know, trying to find out stuff like we all are. Don't you believe he's one of us?"

"How do we know that?" she asked. "And what's us? I don't even know what *you* do here."

Tom looked up quickly. Two men in RAF uniforms were settling themselves at a table across from them. Nancy crooked her head as a signal for her and Tom to leave. Outside, in the corridor, she turned to him.

"What if he knows who the spies are and isn't telling us?" she said. "He could know everything and yet be working for them. There's the ringleader they are desperate to find, the most dangerous spy of all, Sir said. What if it's him?"

"Oh come off it," said Tom, his voice mocking. "You've seen *one* tiny thing and you've already made up your mind."

She reached over and grabbed his arm. "There's something else," she whispered. Her eyes were now brimming with tears and she leant in closer towards him. "My father was arrested last night," she said.

Tom stared at her. "What for?"

"I don't know; do you?"

"How on earth should I know?"

"Because you know more than you're letting on, that's why," hissed Nancy. "I know you do and I remember you were there when that spy case was first collected from our house. Father's not a spy, if that's what anyone thinks, and I'm going to prove it by unmasking the real spy."

She began walking down the corridor. Within seconds Tom was beside her. They entered Number 10 together. Tom clattered the plotting stick on the nearest table. One of the Wrens looked up and glared at him.

The room was far emptier than usual. Just one ARP warden manned the line of telephones. A single Wren sat by a desk to the side of the lower level. The supervisor sat reading a newspaper. Nancy breezed down the stairs with an air of cheerfulness. Tom was watching from above.

"Hey, anything I need to know about; I mean, that I need to tell them about?" asked Nancy, not knowing quite what she was about.

The supervisor on shift didn't look up from his reading. "And who would be asking now?" he asked quietly.

"I'll be going into the Intercept Room shortly: just wondering if there's, well, there's anything in particular you want me to, ahem, report or, better still, look out for." She was fumbling for words. Her heart had begun to thud and she was convinced the effects would soon be showing in a red flush on her cheeks. But neither he nor the Wren said anything. He continued with his paper; she continued writing.

Nancy walked over to one of the desks on the upper level and sat down, pretending to be waiting for instructions or for something to happen. The supervisor got up out of his seat and stretched his back, yawning loudly. He mumbled something to the Wren, something Nancy didn't catch. She saw the Wren glance up from her work. After stretching, the man walked over to the map. Nancy watched his slow plod before fixing her eyes on the bunch of keys on the side of his desk. The man yawned again and continued his slow progress around the map, eventually coming to a stop beneath the desk at which the ARP man sat. He looked up and the two men began to speak. They spoke in normal tones, but Nancy was too preoccupied to listen. She slowly raised herself up from her desk and crept down the stairs. She looked over towards the two men. The ARP uniform was reaching into the drawer by his side and pulled out an envelope. He opened it deliberately, watching the other man's face for a response.

"By golly, where'd ya get those?" said the supervisor with glee in his voice.

The Wren looked up and what she saw was enough to prompt her to stand up and join the others. "A bit of contraband is it?" she said in a playful tone.

"No, not a bit of it," said the ARP warden; "I'm just careful, that's all. The wife said they'd see me though a rough shift and they might yet."

"Bring 'em out here and you'll have a riot on your hands," said the Wren.

The three of them huddled closer together, their heads pointing downwards towards the much-admired item. Nancy watched them. Tom was studying her as if to ask what she was doing. Nancy turned her back to him and moved closer to the supervisor's desk. The bunch of keys hung from a nail on the side of the desk. She shifted her body so as to obscure the keys from their line of view. Next she reached behind her to fumble for the bunch, lifting them and putting them in her left pocket. She knew she did not have long to act, and so she made her way back up the stairs and outside the door. It wasn't until she was at the top of the stairs that she saw they were, in fact, admiring two tiny lumps of white sugar that the ARP warden had produced from the envelope.

Nancy raced along the corridor, away from the direction of the main entrance. There were footsteps behind, it was Tom. He caught up with her and grabbed her arm. "What on earth are you doing now?" he whispered.

She shrugged herself out of his grasp but said nothing.

She knew where Peach had his office. Once she had been tasked with fetching him for a briefing in Number 10. She came up to it and fumbled for a key. She tried several in the lock until the mechanism moved with a heavy, weary clunk. Footsteps could be heard in the corridor and she flung the door open and ran inside. Tom followed, leaving the door ajar.

"Isn't there a light?" asked Tom. He fumbled along the wall until he found a small switch. The light was dim but enough for them to see and to shut the door properly behind them.

"Now what are you doing? You'll get us thrown out of here for good!" Tom was angry, but Nancy could also see that he was thrilled to be a part of something.

"I have to know what he's up to and who he's really working for," she said in a whisper.

"And this is the answer?" Tom glanced around the room. "Look at it; it's an almighty mess."

He was right. Boxes and filing cabinets had been crammed around a single desk which itself was awash with papers and files. Nancy hardly knew why she had forced her way in here or even what she was looking for. "We have to start somewhere," she said.

She found herself being drawn towards the desk. Papers and envelopes had spewed out of a tray and over the desk and telephone until they had fallen into the chair and onto the floor. She reached out and lifted some of the papers but there was nothing beneath. Beside her, Tom began to rummage around. He went to take another step but banged his foot against something hidden underneath a stack of newspapers. He let out a yelp before kicking the papers away. Underneath was a simple cardboard box. It looked flimsy but must have been full of something hard enough to hurt Tom's foot. He reached down and opened the lid.

"It's just books," he said. "Wait a second: what's this?" He had lifted a thick volume out of the box and was holding it up. The cover was a burgundy colour and very plain. Tom opened it and began to flip through. "By golly, it's German; I'm sure of it," he said.

"Let me see." Nancy reached across to take it.

"Hold on, hold on," said Tom, swinging his body away from her. He attempted to read a page. "I suppose it helped them translate the Morse messages before they started using codes."

He passed her the book and swung down to take another out of the box. "Here's another one," he said. "This isn't a language book, though: look, it's got pictures of Germany in it. Maybe it's to find out more about the enemy, their tactics and stuff."

Nancy's eyes suddenly fell on something she recognised. In the corner of the room stood a black suitcase. She went over to it and stooped down. "Help me with this," she said.

Together they lifted it onto Peach's desk. Nancy released the clasps and opened the top. Inside were the same coils and dials as she had seen on her first day at Megg House. It was undoubtedly the spy radio set from her own family privy, discovered so many weeks ago.

"Is that the one?" asked Tom, leaning in.

"Yes, it's the same, I'm sure of it," said Nancy.

"What's he doing with it?" asked Tom.

"Search me, I mean what use is it to him?"

They both leant over the suitcase. Just then Nancy noticed something she hadn't seen before. It was the corner of a piece of paper wedged between the set and the edge of the case. She reached over and pulled it out. What she read astonished her. For typed upon it was a frequency followed by a simple Morse code message, written down.

"What does it say?" asked Tom.

"It's a frequency and a callsign," she said. "I know this, I know this, it's the same one I intercept."

"Show me," said Tom, reaching out his hand.

She handed the paper to him.

"Are you sure?" he asked.

"Certain. What do you think I've been doing for weeks?"

"Okay, okay, just asking," he said, handing the paper back to her.

"Do you realise what this means?" asked Nancy. "Peach has the set and he has the frequency and the callsign. What if it's him sending the messages? What if he's one of *them*."

She couldn't even bring herself to say the word spy. It was too horrible a thought. They both stood staring at each other for a moment. The unspoken idea that Peach was a German spy seemed to hang in the air between them. But, then, the moment was broken by a voice in the corridor. What's more, it appeared to be close to the door.

"It's Peach," said Tom.

The voice became louder. Nancy and Tom looked at each other in panic. There was nowhere to escape, no excuse that could be given. It grew louder again and stopped outside the door. Yes, the voice definitely belonged to Peach. They heard it again and it was then joined by a second. It was followed by footsteps.

"He's gone off somewhere," Tom whispered. "We've got to get out of here."

Nancy slammed the top of the suitcase down. She and Tom hurled it off the table and shoved it back in the corner along with the box of German books. Next they made for the door. The corridor outside was empty. Nancy fumbled with the keys. She shoved the key into the lock but it jammed and wouldn't turn.

"Hurry up," pleaded Tom.

She went to turn the key again when she heard the voice coming back down the corridor. It was Peach returning. She tried once more but still the lock wouldn't move. Her hands began to sweat. The voice grew louder and any moment he would be in sight.

Nancy leant forward and used all her desperate strength to turn the key. Finally the lock mechanism moved with a clunk. She pulled out the key and shoved the bunch into her pocket just as she saw Peach round the corner. A few more footsteps brought him to where they stood.

He took a moment to study their faces before he spoke. "Coming to see me?" he asked. He looked serious, even suspicious.

"I wanted to know if you have anything for me to do; it's a bit quiet today," Nancy blurted out.

Peach looked at her carefully. Several tense moments passed. Eventually he said: "Wait here." He pulled out his key and unlocked his office door. Going inside, he shut the door behind him. After a couple of minutes he re-emerged frowning. "I'm glad you're here, Nancy, as there is something I want you to see," he said, his back to her as he relocked the door. He turned to Tom. "Don't you have work to do?"

Tom's face reddened. "Ahem, yeah I suppose."

"Then be a good lad and get on with it," said Peach.

Tom hesitated. He looked towards Nancy before he shrugged his shoulders and began to walk down the corridor. Peach turned back to Nancy.

"This will take a few hours but it will be worth it, I promise. You up for it or do you have something more pressing to do?"

"No, no." Nancy fumbled for her words. He was looking at her as he had never done before.

"Great," said Peach, "Come with me then." He took her arm and they began to walk away. "Just need to pop into Number 10 to pick up any last-minute intercepts," he said as they rounded the corner.

Nancy scanned Number 10 for Tom but he was not there and it was still quiet. She watched as Peach spoke and flirted with the young Wren; both had their backs to her. Carefully she seized her opportunity and drew the keys from her pocket and placed them back on the nail she had taken them from. Relieved, she then waited for Peach to finish whatever he was doing.

STATION X

1940

"I've a car waiting," said Peach as they stepped outside. He waved her into the front passenger seat before he got in beside her. Just as he started the engine Nancy saw a Wren run out of the front door. She was waving a piece of paper around in her hand. Peach opened the door and took it from her.

"One more: might prove useful, sir," she said.

"Thank you, Betty my love," said Peach with a smile.

They pulled away from Megg House and down the drive. Nancy looked across. He was looking forward, his expression fixed. "Where are we going?" she asked. She felt very uneasy.

"Ah now, you're allowed to see this place, but you mustn't let on to anyone you even know this place exists," he said without turning to look at her.

The route took them out onto the main road and into the countryside. Peach offered no explanation as to where they were heading or how long it would take to get there. Feeling somewhat like a prisoner, Nancy spent much of the journey looking out at the world outside the window. Occasionally she would glance over at Peach, but he rarely glanced back. She watched the hedgerows and fields swish by and fixed her eyes on the horizon. She was in agony. How was she to confront him? What was she to say? And how on earth would she get anyone to believe her? If he suspected her was she even safe?

Every so often Peach would give a comment on the landscape but most of the journey was spent in silence. It lasted almost three hours, including several stops to refuel.

Eventually they came to a gate by the side of a country lane. Nancy saw two guards, both carrying large guns, approach the car. Peach wound down the window and passed one of the guards an envelope. The guard opened it and unfolded a piece of paper, which he quickly read before handing it back. The guard motioned for the barrier to be lifted and soon they were being waved through. The drive swept before them and to her right Nancy saw a wide, glass-like lake surrounded by bushes and trees. They circled a sharp bend and to the left a villa came into view. It was a building of brown brick and whitewash containing a series of bay windows and arched gables. To Nancy's eyes it was at least two storeys high and had a large, arched entrance, not quite central, in the front façade. The car stopped outside the door. Peach was the first to spring out. He motioned for Nancy to follow.

To her surprise another guard met them at the door. Peach produced some paperwork from his top pocket and the guard quickly stepped aside. Just a few steps led them into a hallway not at all unlike that at Megg House. The carpet was thick and the wood panelling dark. Nancy quickly realised that it was, in effect, just an ante-room, for Peach quickly made for a door at the other side. He led her into another hallway, bigger than the first, with a staircase, at the foot of which sat a crisply uniformed man behind a desk. He looked up at Peach with an expression of unsmiling recognition.

"More intercepts from the North?" he asked.

"The Midlands, as you well know," joked Peach. The man's expression remained blank. Peach cleared his throat and retrieved a file from under his arm. "Yes, more intercepts from Station M."

The man behind the desk sighed heavily. He picked up a telephone receiver and dialled. "Ask someone from one of the huts to receive some intercepts from the main house, will you?" he said. The voice must have asked something in enquiry, for he replied, "Station M, no M, that's right."

The man replaced the receiver and looked up, first at Peach and then at Nancy, as if he'd only just been made aware of her presence. "Someone will be with you shortly," he said.

"I'm much obliged," replied Peach.

Nancy heard voices descending the stairs. Soon a group of around twenty people, mainly women, filled the hallway. The ladies' dresses were plain, their hair carefully arranged and their nails and lips coloured. They crowded around the desk, each talking to the man behind it and to each other. Then, through the crowd, an older man, also in plain clothes, approached Peach. He was reduced to virtually shouting over the clamour of the group.

"Come over to Hut Six," he yelled.

"Can I bring her?" Peach motioned towards Nancy. "She's important to our work, I can promise you that."

"Has she signed the Act?" asked the man.

"Oh yes, yes, she's fully integrated into the work at Station M."

The man gave a sharp nod of consent and led them back out of the front doors, immediately turning sharply to the left. He walked at a galloping pace and Nancy had to skip to keep up. She felt a tug on her arm. It was Peach. He leant down to speak in her ear. "You haven't seen any of this, remember?" he said.

"No more than I've seen anything at Megg House," she said.

They walked past the side of the house and up a slight incline. It was then that Nancy saw the wooden huts stretched out before her. It was like another version of Megg House. They came to a small-looking hut and entered. What Nancy saw resembled a classroom. There were rows of wooden desks, behind which sat men and women studying paperwork and chewing pencils. A blackboard had been placed at one end of the room. As they entered a young man, no more than twenty-five, approached them. His arm was outstretched towards Peach and his eyes creased in a smile.

"So you bring us more work, as if we're not busy enough eh?" He spoke in an accent Nancy did not recognise.

"More work for you and for us," said Peach, opening the file. "We've intercepted what we think is HQ in Germany communicating with the spies on the ground, but the spies aren't communicating back all that much."

"Is that a surprise to you, given the circumstances?" replied the young man. "Most communications are on a strict basis of, what's the word, necessity, is that it? They receive their instructions and get on with it."

"But wouldn't the German HQ need to know what they're planning?"

"Not necessarily. They're given free rein to get on with the job. After all, we can expect them to be highly organized and trained, can we not? They will proceed as they see fit. German HQ may be issuing basic instructions or information as to future air strikes. Or it could be something else entirely."

Peach handed over the file. "It's encrypted, five letter codes," he said, sighing deeply. "If they're using Enigma or some other system there's not much hope of finding out what it says, is there?"

The man smiled back. "In here, there is always hope," he said. "A simple mistake here, a repeat there, a sign-off, a greeting, all of these can break the normal rules of the code and tell us more. We put it all together and, well, we have something of a surprise for you."

He drew away from them and turned towards a large desk at the far side of the room. Peach shouted after him. "We've been pinning our hopes on tracking them via the signals themselves rather than the messages, but even that is cut off from us."

"But probably not forever," came the reply. "In the meantime, if these messages tell us something more about the German's forward planning, all the better for us."

"Are you really expecting them to?"

"We expect nothing and look for everything."

He was walking back towards them. Nancy noticed he was smiling. He handed Peach a small file. "Not everyone is using Enigma and that gives us, well, a few shortcuts here and there."

"What do you mean?" asked Peach. The man nodded and continued to smile.

Peach opened the file. After a few seconds he looked up at the man. "Is this for real?"

"Like I said, not everything is Enigma and not everything is unreadable, at least not to us."

Peach took a step towards him. "How many have you decrypted?"

"Not many, as you see, but enough to give you something to work on, for now at least."

"And when were you planning to tell us, we've been straining…"

"Just this morning, I can assure you, but I knew you were coming and I just couldn't resist delivering the news in person. Now take that back, and if we learn anything more you will be the first to know."

They retreated from the hut and began to make their way towards the car, not bothering to go back into the house. Once inside the car, Peach sat in the driving seat, as before, with Nancy at his side. She was shocked to see that he was trembling. His skin had turned white and he stared straight ahead, his hands rigid on the steering wheel. They sat in silence until Nancy butted in.

"Where are we?" she asked.

Peach said nothing but continued to stare out of the driver's window. She asked again. Eventually he relaxed and drew himself back into his seat. "We're at Station X, and for goodness' sake don't tell anyone I brought you here."

"But why have you given them our intercepts?" asked Nancy.

"Their job is to decrypt them, find out what they say."

"And have they?"

"Yes they have, they well and truly have."

He pulled open the file again and read it thoroughly. "Good lord," he said after a while; "Good lord, I think they're onto them."

"Onto them, how?" asked Nancy.

"Well they've run into something, that's for sure." He looked up at her. "This could be it. This could be the breakthrough we've been looking for."

He carefully placed the folder on the back seat. Nancy expected him to start up the engine, but he did not. Instead, they sat in silence. The tension in the car on the drive down had been difficult, but now it was unbearable. She stared ahead, watching the guards walk back and forth across the gate. When they were inside Station X Nancy had managed to push her discoveries about Peach into the background, but now she was alone with him again she was reminded of the possible threat to herself and many others. But he had seemed so enthusiastic just now. Talking to the men in the hut he had appeared eager to catch the spies. Maybe she was wrong about him; maybe he was just following orders and watching Miss Temple, trying to gain her confidence and have her lead him to the most dangerous spy, the ringleader. But if so, why had he seemed so worried when they had returned to the car?

"Where did you think I was going on the motorbike all those times?" Peach's voice jolted her. He was staring at her now.

"We're not the only ones doing what we do. There are others, a lot of others. The messages end up here; well, a lot of them do. Everything is part of a bigger puzzle, one they're putting together here."

He looked over towards the house. "I'd love to know everything they're really doing here," he said, his tone suddenly quieter than before. "But I have a feeling about this place. I reckon this is where the War is really being fought. This is where it'll be won, or lost. Not out there: well, there as well, but *here...*" His voice trailed off.

"Why have you brought me here?" Nancy blurted out.

"Because I want to talk to you and I want you to understand."

"Understand what?"

"The bigger picture, that's what."

He swivelled around in his seat, his upper body facing hers. "We all hear things and we all see things and sometimes we think we understand what they mean, but in this War we are only seeing a tiny part, our tiny part, of things. The important thing is that we get on with our job and let others get on with theirs. If we start to do more we risk stepping into things that are none of our concern, do you understand?"

"What if we see something that others need to know about?"

"Then tell them, but it's up to those above you to decide what action to take. It's all about the bigger picture and it's all about trust. Step out of line and you risk wandering into something that doesn't concern you, something that could get you, or others, hurt, or even killed."

He turned back to face the windscreen. He murmured something and then said it again.

"After all we don't want the wrong people to be arrested, do we?"

Nancy felt a cold shiver through her entire body. What did he mean? Father? Had he been the one to have him arrested? Was it a warning to her, telling her to stop interfering, stop asking any questions? She went to say something but her mouth refused to open. Her heart pounding, she clutched the sides of the seat and stared ahead. Peach started the car and began to pull away slowly. "And no-one wants that to happen, especially me," he said, almost to himself.

They drove through the gates and back out onto the country lane. Just as the car was picking up speed Nancy spotted the back of a sign. She craned her neck to read what it said as they passed. It was a single word, the name of a village she assumed. It was a strange name, one she had not heard before. It was called Bletchley.

THE LIBRARY

2010

Arthur jumped out of the car while Mum fumbled for change to pay for the parking ticket. There was only a week left of the summer holidays and Mum was on a mission to stock him up with clothes and stationery. They walked together, past Orethorpe Magistrates' Court, with its filthy Victorian brickwork, a boarded-up kebab kiosk and two charity shops. Taking large strides along the road, Arthur saw the familiar widening of the pavement in front of him, the slabs changing, becoming large and smooth, as they led to the Langleys Shopping Centre.

The shops were arranged around a large square. The shop facades were made of heavy brick. They stretched several storeys high. The windows were full of mannequins dressed in shorts and bikinis and glaring posters displaying giant heads, feet, hands, teeth, scrawny models in bras and pants, mobile phones, cappuccinos and diamonds rings. A small area of flowers and bushes had been planted in the centre of the square. They surrounded a great brass sculpture of men and women, ten feet tall. All the figures leant into the centre, their heads bowed and their backs to everyone else. Brass overalls had been carved over their bodies, thick boots on their feet. In the centre, sprouting above their heads, was a huge aeroplane wing. A single plaque stood nearby: *Langleys, British Aircraft Manufacturer, 1910-1982.*

Before today Arthur had asked his mother who the statues were supposed to represent. "Factory workers; this place used to be a huge factory," she had said. "Hundreds of people worked here, thousands, during the War."

Arthur hated shopping, especially when it required him to try on clothes and parade up and down while Mother inspected the cut of the jacket and the width of the shoes. Afterwards, by way of a reward, she treated him to a burger.

"Can I stay for a bit? I want to have a look round." asked Arthur as they stood up to leave.

Mother looked at him curiously. "Whatever for? You hate shopping!"

"It's not shopping. Some of the lads said they'd be hanging around later, that's all."

She picked up her bags. "Well okay, but I don't want you hanging around all day; you'll get bored, and that's when trouble starts. Dad will pick you up around four."

He watched her leave, the shopping bags banging against her legs. He then turned towards the square and walked past the shops. There was a small row of buildings set aside from the main square. There was a dentist, a solicitor's office and a sports injury centre, although Arthur didn't actually know what that meant. Passing them, he saw what he wanted straight ahead. The new town library had been opened five years before, and its glass entrance and new brickwork stood out.

He went inside and walked straight to the reception desk. A young woman looked up. "We're closing early today," she said.

"But this won't take long," said Arthur. "I want to look something up: is there a computer free?"

She got up and went over to a line of computer desks. "How long do you want it for?"

"Only ten minutes, but I need some help with it."

"With what?"

"I want to look something up, but I might need a bit of help understanding."

She beckoned him to sit down behind a computer screen. Leaning over, she asked: "I can help now if it won't take long. What is it?"

Arthur pulled the piece of paper from his trouser pocket, the one he had scribbled on in Mr Smith's house. The words *Gacek, Studio fotograficzne Dunajski, Warszawa, 1889* were written upon it. These were the words printed on the back of the group photograph. Next to it he had scribbled the words *Albert Schmitt, 1918*, the words on the back of the photograph of the young man in uniform.

"I want to know what these words mean," he said to the assistant, handing the paper to her.

She glanced down at it and leant over the screen. Holding the mouse, she brought an internet search engine page up onto the screen and began to tap out the words on the keyboard.

"Well 'Gacek' is a Polish surname by the look of it," she said.

"Polish?"

"Well, yes, and that makes sense because you see this word 'Warszawa'? That's Polish for Warsaw."

"What's Warsaw? I mean, I've heard of it but I don't know where it is."

"It's the capital of Poland, the European country of Poland."

Her fingers lightly tapped the keyboard and the screen filled with pictures of modern skyscrapers, an old-looking town square and an ancient clock face. Scrolling down, the photographs changed to show images of bombed-out buildings standing against a winter sky.

She turned back to him. "Where did you see these words?" she asked.

"I saw them on an old photograph and wondered what they were."

"Well it was taken in Warsaw in 1889, and you see here, 'Studio fotograficzne Dunajski', that's the name of the photographic studio. A family picture, was it?"

"Yeah, a load of people together."

"Well that must be the Gacek family then. What else is there?"

"Albert Schmitt, 1918."

"Well we don't need the internet for that; it's a German name."

Arthur looked up. "German?"

"Yes, certainly. What was the picture of?"

"A man in uniform."

"Well, it could be a young German solider from the First World War." She straightened upright and peered down. "A school project, is it?" she asked.

"No, not exactly, it's just something I saw and I didn't recognise the names." He stood up, not wanting to be asked any more questions. "Mystery solved; thank you for all your help."

"You're welcome." She was leaning over the keyboard again and clicking the mouse to shut down the internet site. Arthur left her to it and began to walk towards the exit. The first set of automatic glass doors opened and he was crossing the small hallway when he noticed that a side-room door was open. Outside, close to him, were two large posters showing black and white images. They reminded him of what he'd just seen. One was the remains of a house, its front crumpled into rubble. Standing beside it were several men in old-fashioned-looking dress and hard hats. The other image was also black and white, but Arthur could see it showed rows and rows of terraced houses surrounding a big, flat area from which black smoke billowed. He decided to investigate further. A woman his grandmother's age was seated inside.

"Welcome to the exhibition, although I must warn you we're closing in ten minutes," she said.

"An exhibition of what?" asked Arthur.

"These all around the walls," she was pointing, "they're all photographs telling the story of Orethorpe during the Second World War. And beneath them, you see, there's some information as well. Feel free to have a look, and if you're interested we're having a much bigger exhibition up at the main house over Christmas and New Year."

Arthur didn't know what she meant by the 'main house' or the bombing anniversary but he liked the photographs and so walked up to the nearest one. It, like the one outside, showed the remains of a large house. Its front had caved in but you could still see the different floors of the house. It reminded Arthur of pictures of dolls' houses. Beside it was a photograph showing a row of people, mainly women, queuing beside a butcher's shop. Arthur went around the room, scanning the photographs in turn. There was an image of a train packed full of men in uniform, some leaning out of the windows, kissing women lined along the platform. There was a close-up of a boy, no more than ten, wearing a helmet with the letters ARP on it. He had freckles and was grinning into the camera. And there was one of an old manor house with its large drive and lawn, and beside this photograph another showing an old hut: "rather like a shed" thought Arthur. Another, smaller image was of men and women in a large room full of desks. Some sat at typewriters; others were chewing on pencils or looking down at some paperwork in front of them. And there was an even smaller, low-quality photograph of what looked like a large aerial planted into some ground. Arthur stopped to read the inscriptions. *Megg House played a vital part in the town's War effort, but its role was kept highly secret and it is only now that we are starting to learn more, thanks to the declassification of several key reports and documents.*

"We're looking for more on that place." Arthur hadn't noticed the woman standing beside him, and her voice made him jump. "Sorry, dear, I didn't mean to startle you," she said.

"That's okay. What's Megg House?"

"It's an old people's home now, but we think it was some kind of secret intelligence base during the War. What I wanted to say was, if you come across anyone who might know anything about it or know someone who worked there, please ask them to get in touch with the Orethorpe Heritage Association, as we're desperate for more information."

"What, do you mean secret intelligence?"

"Well you've heard of Bletchley Park, haven't you, where the German codes were smashed? We think Megg House might have been involved in that and maybe even more. I even had someone in here the other day claiming they'd been trying to catch spies." Even though she was so much older than him, the woman was barely taller than Arthur himself. She smiled across at him and he smiled back.

"My mum and dad only moved here after they got married, so I don't have family nearby," he said. "But I can ask the history teacher at school when I get back."

"You do that, dear," she said turning back towards the photographs. "It would be so nice to know more. Who knows, it could put Orethorpe back on the map."

A BREAKTHROUGH

1940

Shortly after they returned from Bletchley to Megg House, Nancy was led down the back corridors and outside into the grounds. Sir grabbed the file from Peach with both hands and read it eagerly. Now she was following them both across the uneven grass towards the lights of one of the outside huts. Once inside everyone was asked to gather in the centre of the room where Peach stood alongside Sir. Peach was the first to speak up. He held a file aloft for all to see.

"This is a message sent from Orethorpe to Germany last week and intercepted by us. Something incredible has happened. Station X has managed to decipher it, and not only this one but several others as well."

A loud cheer went up in the room. The women were smiling and clapping and the men began to drum the tables with their hands. Peach raised his hands to return everyone to silence.

Sir stepped forward. "Message number one, transmitted at 0713 hours precisely a week ago." He began to write on a board behind him.

"The messages reads, '*Activity in target 1 quickening, suggesting further shipments expect...*"

"What is target one?" asked a Wren.

"We assume it to be one of the factories," replied Peach.

Sir continued. "The second message reads thus," he reached out to write on the board again.

"*Disruption possible. Must act quickly. Cannot wait for more agents. Respond.*""

"The third message is the most telling," said Peach.

Sir leant forward and wrote out a series of coordinates on the board. "The third message is simply coordinates which, we believe, identify the target," he said. "Ladies and gentleman, these coordinates lead us to one place: Langleys factory. It's the largest factory and it's near completion of its latest, shall we say, its latest order. It makes sense."

Nancy felt her legs begin to shake. At that very moment Father and Audrey would be working on the assembly line, in the warehouses or at a desk: they and thousands of others.

"The spies are asking for the bombers to come back?" asked one of the men in uniform.

"We're assuming this doesn't relate to German bombers," said Sir, shaking his head. "The bombers have already damaged a couple of the factories, we know. I believe this is referring to another deliberate, targeted attack by the spies themselves, on the ground, one that can be delivered with precision. Look at what it says: '*Disruption possible. Must act quickly.*' They're primed and ready."

The murmuring began again, until Sir interrupted. "Some of you may know people working at Langleys; you may even have relatives there, so I must remind you that this information is strictly classified. I will do my best to protect it and the many people working there, but you cannot, and must not, repeat what you hear in this room. To do otherwise would be classed as an act of treason, understood?"

Everyone nodded in silence. The moment for joy and relief had passed.

There wasn't much more for Nancy to do except return to work. But the Intercept Room was a frustrating place, for the wires were silent of enemy agents that day, as they were most days. Eventually Miss Halsall came to ask if she wanted a break with her. Nancy was grateful for the invitation. As they were making their way across the corridor they passed outside Sir's office. Sir was standing behind his desk, Peach across from him. They looked tense, even panicked.

"It couldn't be worse," said Sir.

"You mean the, ahem, the delivery, Sir?"

"Yes of course, it's top priority isn't it?" shouted Sir.

"But this doesn't mean they know about, you know."

"Why else target Langleys?"

Just then Sir caught sight of Nancy and Miss Halsall glancing across. He shot a glance towards Peach. In response, Peach reached out his foot and kicked the door shut.

WAITING

1940

The fear and uncertainty were now greater than anything Nancy had known before, and they grew daily. She had not told Sir what she had seen outside Miss Temple's house. What was the point? Peach would only say he was trying to extract information. And what about the suitcase in his room, should she tell him about that? Tom had talked her out of it. "He'll only say it's being used for intelligence," he had said.

"Oh yes, and what about the frequency? It's still in use. That points the finger at him."

"No it doesn't. They already know about the frequency. For goodness' sake, they've got you monitoring the frequency haven't they? If he really was a spy he'd tell the others to stop using it. He'd tell them, the spies, that they're being listened to."

"You don't believe me do you, about him being part of this?" asked Nancy.

"To be honest, no I don't," said Tom. "You're letting your imagination run away with you and you've got no proof, no proof at all. Besides, Sir trusts him doesn't he?"

At least there Tom was right. She had no proof, and Sir did trust Peach, unquestionably. No, she would need more evidence before she told Sir.

Several days had passed since their return from Station X but Peach was nowhere to be seen. She soon knew why. That afternoon Sir drove her into town. Approaching Langleys, Nancy saw a new barrier across the road. A man she recognised as a young junior officer from Megg House approached the car. Sir wound down his window as the officer saluted.

"The extra security for the factory has all been arranged, Sir. Peach is up by the gates if you need a word with him."

"Now he's just the person I want to see," said Sir.

They drove on. Further barriers had been put up along both sides of the road. Men in various uniforms had been stationed along the route. Approaching the main gates, Nancy saw Army privates standing either side. Each one held a rifle. A small group stood to the side. Sir stopped the car and got out. Nancy decided to follow. Sir approached the group and someone in a heavy overcoat swung around. It was Peach. He gave a stiff salute.

"Any updates on the delivery?" asked Sir, one of his eyebrows arching as he spoke.

"We're discussing that now, Sir."

"We need to get the stuff away as soon as possible and during the daylight. I never thought it was a good idea to move it at night. It gives the cover of darkness to those wanting to steal or damage it."

"Yes, Sir, but you know it wasn't our call to make. It still isn't."

"It has to be soon."

"Yes, Sir, agreed."

Sir and Nancy got back into the car. "We're convinced that whatever they're planning is connected with the next delivery from this factory, and that's imminent," said Sir. "Peach is overseeing the operation. The sooner that stuff is out and where it needs to be, the sooner we can all sleep easier, eh?"

"Yes, Sir," said Nancy. She wondered what was to be delivered and why it was so important.

They drove along in silence but Nancy's head was swimming with questions. "What about that man I saw in the woods: why can't you find him?" she finally blurted out.

"There are thousands of men that match his description," said Sir, his voice calm.

"Well, what about the house, then, where Miss Temple lives? Peach said it would be watched."

"And it was. The man disappeared without trace and the schoolteacher hasn't seen him since; both Peach and I are convinced of it. No-one knows anything about him."

"Someone might," thought Nancy, her thoughts drifting back to the sight of Peach entering the woman's house and her cheerfully climbing into his car.

THE DANCE

1940

School finished two weeks before Christmas on account of the coal shortages. The week of Christmas arrived and with it the of the town hall dance. For one night the hall was to become a place of celebration, of joy even, almost as if the War had been won or had never even broken out in the first place.

At 8 o'clock on the night, Nancy, Mary, Kep, Mother and Father picked their way across the cobbles of the old street. A crowd had gathered around the corner of the road, and she soon realised why: the queue from the hall was down the street. They took their places at the back.

Young men in uniform and young women with bright fingernails and lips chatted and laughed. Older couples stood in silence; the men shifting and stamping their feet; the women looking ahead. Nancy caught sight of someone frantically waving, beckoning them forward. The party of five left their place and walked down the queue to where Mrs Harris was waiting. "Come in with us, my dear, no need to get chilled to the bone," said Mrs Harris to Mother, adding: "We don't want your legs all seized up on the dance floor, do we?" She let out a loud laugh.

They began inching their way closer to the double doors of the hall. Stepping through them, Nancy saw that rows of red and green paper strips tightly woven together into rope had been hung on the bare walls and across the ceiling of the small reception area. Before long she and the others were carried by the crowd into the main room. Here more paper streamers of varying colours hung along the ceiling and down the walls. Wooden tables and chairs stood around the dance floor, each table holding a candle in a jam jar. The band sat next to the far wall, some in uniform and others in their best suits. They stared out across the expanse of polished floorboards and onto the groups which were now crowding into the room.

Nancy felt a tug on her arm. Kep appeared at her side. "I'm just settling the parents and Mary over by the corner," he said. He gently guided her through the swelling groups and towards the table to the right of the dance floor. Father stood behind Mother's chair, helping her remove her coat.

"Now I'm sorted with the two most beautiful girls," said Kep as he pulled out a chair for Nancy. Mrs Harris stopped talking and looked over sharply. "Don't let your sister hear you say that," she said.

Kep sat down. "Sisters don't count," he said, flashing a warm smile over to Nancy.

Kep looked up and smiled at someone behind her. Nancy looked around to see Joyce with her two other brothers. Both were younger and looked uncomfortable in their shirts and ties. Behind them stood

Jack Jones, the Harrises' lodger. "Go and find somewhere and behave," Mrs Harris shouted across at them.

"I don't need a seat; I'll be too busy dancing," said Joyce with glee.

Just as she was moving away, Nancy's focus came to rest on a large group swelling into the room behind them. At the front was Audrey, arm in arm with the man Nancy knew as Joseph, her sister's supervisor at the factory. Audrey's long hair had been released from the clips and net that usually held it together during her shifts. It shone and gleamed as Audrey's head went from side-to-side, her eyes darting around the room. They briefly came to rest on her family. Nancy saw her sister give them a smile and a nod before the group moved on to the other side of the room. Nancy turned back to the table. As usual, her elder sister had irritated her, and once again she was angry at herself for it.

For several minutes she sat in silence. Mother and Mrs Harris chattered away, not noticing Father sat between them, his legs crossed and his eyes staring forward. Across the table Kep and Mary sat with their shoulders and arms touching, their hands clasped tightly together. There was a loud clatter of a cymbal falling to the ground, laughter from the crowd and then a round of applause. Looking around, Nancy saw that an older-looking man with red cheeks had stepped onto the dance floor. He bowed briefly to his eager audience before turning his back to face the band. The musicians looked at him expectantly, like a dog awaiting its food. Then, as he lifted his arms, they began their chorus of music.

"There's something very unnatural about dancing," Nancy said to herself. Opposite her on the dance floor was Henry, one of Joyce's brothers. They were swaying to some kind of low-key song, or at least they were trying to, but the close presence of so many other couples swelling the dance floor had turned what was supposed to be a beehive of organised motion into something resembling a herd of cows being jostled down a country lane to be milked. Conversation was useless over the din so they continued, in silence, trying to sway virtually on the spot. Swapping places with Henry she surveyed the opposite side of the room. A flash of a light caught her eye and Nancy glanced up towards the back wall. A woman dressed in dark clothing held a cosmetic mirror close to her face. As she lowered her hand, her face came into full view. Nancy recognised her immediately. It was Miss Temple.

She was slouched slightly, her right leg bent, the foot resting on the wall behind her. All the time her head kept moving from left to right, her eyes skipping across the groups, the tables, the swirling feet and grinning faces.

Henry leant in to shout something into Nancy's ear. She wriggled away from him, keeping her eyes on the schoolteacher in the corner. Henry looked across as well. "Who's she then?" he shouted at Nancy.

She turned towards him, bringing them face-to-face. "One of my schoolteachers," she replied.

A uniformed man in his twenties had attempted to swing his partner over towards them, sending her almost into Henry's arms. The woman laughed loudly. "Keep moving: it's a dance floor, not a bus stop," the man shouted over his shoulder as he twisted his partner away from them.

As the dance finished Nancy took two steps off the floor and onto the thick, flowery carpet, close to

Audrey's table. She looked up again. Miss Temple had disappeared. Nancy nudged her way along the edge of the dance floor. A crowd was standing between the dancing couples and the entrance, and she squeezed and pushed her way through the herd of bodies. When she emerged she found she was in the entrance lobby. Then it was her turn to be nudged. Miss Temple came up behind her and didn't bother to slow down as she swerved past, bumping her shoulder against hers. Nancy watched as the woman walked out into the night.

Nancy followed her outside, ignoring the protesting sounds of the ushers warning her of the freezing cold. Miss Temple was leaning against a wall. Her head was tilted upright, her eyes gazing ahead. Great clouds of air came out of her nostrils in the cold night air.

Nancy stood by the doorway, staring, but Miss Temple was either too distracted to notice or too calculating to show that she realised she was being watched.

A car door suddenly slammed. It came from across the road. Someone else Nancy recognised was coming towards her. It was Sir. He was in full uniform, his expression stern. He walked up to Nancy, holding out his hand. He grabbed her arm and swung her back inside. Sir led her inside the dance hall. Entering the din of noise, she shouted at him. "Miss Temple, you know, the schoolteacher, is outside. She has something to do with this, I know she does." She began to tug on his arm but he was unmovable.

A slight smile warmed his features and he looked down upon her. He glanced over her towards the doors. Nancy thought he was going to go outside again, until she saw a young Wren stood close to them. Sir said something to the woman before turning back to Nancy. "Like a dance, do you?" he bellowed. She didn't get to reply for he had caught hold of her arm again and was leading her onto the dance floor. The uniformed men and women parted to let them through. The men saluted and the women threw Nancy curious glances. Sir wrapped his arm around her waist. He took her right hand in his and they began to move. Soon the background of the room became a swirl of colours before Nancy's eyes. Sir's grip on her was strong and their movement unstoppable. Every so often he would look down on her, but most of the time his gaze spun around the room rotating about them. The music grew louder and faster as they went near the band. Sir began to rotate them around quicker than before. She felt the muscles in his arm around her flex and tense; his hand gripped hers even harder.

After several minutes the conductor began to move his arms in slow semi-circles, telling them the tune was about to end. Nancy looked up to see the Wren standing on the edge of the dance floor, tall, statue-like. Sir gripped Nancy's arm again and they began to walk towards the Wren. Seeing them approach, the Wren simply nodded and turned her back to them. They followed her to the edge of the room, close to the foyer. The Wren craned her neck to speak to Sir, but just as he was leaning forward to listen there was a crash from one of the tables along the side of the dance floor. Nancy looked up and instantly saw it came from the direction of her parents' table. There was the sound of raised voices.

"I told you, it was an *accident*; we can all let things *slip*, can't we? Better if it's an *accident* though, isn't it?"

The angry speaker's face was round, the cheeks swollen and red. He wore no uniform, but a brown, cheap-looking jacket over a brown shirt stretched over his heavy stomach.

"You're drunk, man," bellowed Sir.

"And what's it to you, matey?" His eyes narrowed in his fleshy face and although his feet did not move, his upper body swayed from side to side.

"Do you know to whom you speak?" bellowed Sir again.

"*Do you know to whom you speak*?" the man mimicked in a high-pitched voice. He opened his mouth to follow it up with something equally rude, but closed it again when, in that moment, he saw several uniformed men draw closer. Sir turned to one of them. "Take him outside to cool off, but get his name and address before he staggers off," he said to the tall man on his left.

"Right away," came the reply. Moments later he and two other men had grabbed the man and were pushing him towards the doors. Sir reached down and picked up the chair, stood it on its legs, and sat down. He motioned for Mother and Father to do the same. They obeyed meekly. Sir raised his hand and the Wren stepped forward.

"My usual, and get these good people the same again," he said, looking over towards Mother and Father.

Nancy slipped onto a chair at the table. The drinks quickly arrived and it was only minutes before her parents and Sir were exchanging polite comments and questions. Every so often her mother would raise her glass to her lips, take a tiny sip and replace it on the table. Father was less hesitant over his pint. He would take big gulps while nodding and smiling weakly at Sir.

They all sat for several minutes, Sir chattering away. He did not seem to notice the curious and suspicious glances towards the group, towards Nancy's Father. Eventually the gaze of the crowds was drawn away by further arrivals in the room, a fresh round of drinks and the next song.

Finally, Sir drew himself up and stood to his feet. "It's been a pleasure, Mr and Mrs Brown, but I have duties to attend to."

Father went to stand up, but Sir had doffed his hat and walked away before anyone could object. Nancy's eyes followed him to the door. There, Sir stopped in front of a woman. They exchanged no more than a few words. It was Miss Temple again.

The pair parted: Miss Temple into the dance hall, and Sir through the door leading outside. Nancy leapt to her feet and went to follow him. She found him outside in the freezing air.

"Do you know who that was?" she asked, tugging at his sleeve.

"Of course; it's my job to know," he whispered, cocking his head down towards her. "Come with me."

Several steps took them to a waiting car. Sir motioned for Nancy to get in before he climbed into the back seat behind her. No-one spoke until the Wren she had seen earlier climbed into the driver's seat and slammed the door.

"Was that long enough to show support?" asked Sir.

"Yes, Sir," said the Wren.

Sir twisted his back towards the hall. Several stray couples stood outside, chatting and laughing.

"Where to now, Sir?" asked the Wren eventually.

"Langleys, to check on the delivery," he replied.

ROADBLOCK

1940

The car sped down the road towards the factory gates. "What is being delivered?" asked Nancy.

"Weapons and ammunition being sent out from Langleys, stuff that can do a lot of damage in the right hands: and our hands are the right hands, of course."

"But why move them at night?"

"Orders, simple as that. So why do you think the town council decided to throw a dance tonight? We wanted to get as many people as possible out of the way, and if any of the German spies were there then we let them know we aren't afraid to let our people off the leash for a night."

The car was slowing and Sir leant forward. "What's the hold-up?" he asked.

"A roadblock, Sir; they must be moving the stuff now," the Wren called out from the driver's seat.

Nancy was pinned to her seat, her eyes closed and her thoughts drifting back to the sight of Miss Temple at the dance and in the street. She opened her eyes again to see that a type of wooden gate had been draped across the road. Beside it stood some figures she couldn't make out in the dark.

They waited an age. Finally, Sir reached over to open his passenger door. "They should have been through by now," he said. "I'll find out what's going on."

He snapped the door shut behind him and began to walk up to the fuzzy forms in the road. He began speaking to someone. Just then the Wren spoke up. "Sir's getting angry; I wonder why?" she said.

He was standing there in the road with his hands on his hips. He turned his body to the right and raised his elbows. Nancy reached out for the catch on her door and opened it. She stretched out her legs, and as she did so Sir's angry voice reached her. She stepped out of the car and began to walk towards the road block.

"I'm telling you, it won't be long now." The voice came from the man facing Sir. The two men faced each other over the barrier. There was a younger man and a woman, both in uniforms, standing a little way off down the road.

"Get back in the car." Sir's stern voice jolted her. She glanced up at him and at the man he was now shouting at, but said nothing. She turned around and walked away. Back inside the car she waited for him to return.

Some of the drivers behind had begun to get impatient. Several were standing in the road talking and glancing towards Sir and the other people. Just then they swung their heads back at the sound of a giant roar. It was the cry of a car engine being thrashed by its driver. The vehicle pushed on through the black night. It was coming towards them, being driven on the only side of the road that was empty – the wrong side. Nancy saw the bonnet rise and fall as the wheels juddered over the uneven road surface. The men in the road sprang back as it approached. It was not slowing down. Nancy glanced back towards the roadblock and saw Sir and the others staring down the road. The car was almost at the barrier now, but just as it reached the makeshift wooden gate the engine roared again and it smashed through it.

Sir and the others ducked with their hands aloft to protect themselves from the pieces of flying wood. Broken bits fell to the ground just as the speeding car accelerated past the now demolished barrier.

The roadblock guard only gave himself a moment before he turned to the woman behind him. "Withdraw, withdraw!" he shouted.

He raised his rifle and began to draw back, still facing the group. "Get out of here now!" he shouted to the woman. She raised her gun and began to withdraw backwards before turning to run away.

There was a gunshot. The man had fired into the air before he himself rapidly retreated. Nancy heard the Wren open the driver's door to the car and jump out. Nancy watched her run towards Sir. Other men from the cars behind were doing the same. Sir stood motionless and watched the pair run into what looked like a low mist which had begun to seep down the road towards the cars. They disappeared, and it was then that Sir and the Wren began to run after them. Nancy bolted out of the car.

"What's all this about then?" someone asked.

"Did you hear that shot?" shouted another.

Men were shouting to their wives and girlfriends to stay in the cars. Someone came and stood next to Nancy. He went to say something, but instead of taking in a breath to speak he inhaled the first wisps of the dense, bitter fumes that were snaking towards them. He began to cough.

It wasn't fog overcoming them; it was something else. It was too dense, too grey-like to be normal fog or mist, and, it was moving too fast. To Nancy it seemed to be something between liquid and vapour: a thick, stew-like mixture that turned solid as soon as it reached skin, hair, breath and, finally, lungs. "They're gassing us, they're gassing us!" The voice came from behind. They all began to draw back from the toxic cloud, now just a car distance away.

Nancy ran back to the car and scrambled inside. There was a blanket on the back seat and she flung it over her head and held it up to her mouth. Several terrible minutes passed. Then the car jolted and the door opened. The Wren climbed in beside her. Nancy raised the blanket to look. One side of the Wren's face was covered in mud. She too was coughing and retching violently. Seconds later they heard running footsteps. They went past the car, then stopped. The figure turned back towards them and stumbled towards the driver's side, pulled on the door handle and jumped inside. It was Sir.

Less than a minute later the car was racing away. Sir had one hand on the steering wheel; the other held a handkerchief to his mouth. He was gasping for breath, wheezing and coughing furiously. Beside Nancy sat the Wren, in much the same state as she had been when she got back to the car. The car swerved and skidded under Sir's erratic control. Behind them Nancy could see the other cars from the road racing away, just as they were.

They were almost in town when Sir raised his head and withdrew the cloth from his mouth. "It's an ambush," he wheezed. "It wasn't the Home Guard at all: it was them, it was them." He went to cough violently again, but somehow managed to steer the vehicle through the narrow suburbs of the town and out towards Megg House. He began shouting again. "Where did they get those uniforms? Were they going to take the stuff from under our noses or just blow it up in front of everyone? Damn it, damn it."

"What about the car?" Nancy shouted back to him.

"I don't know, but it did us a favour," he shouted back.

Reaching the front of Megg House, Sir did not even bother to switch off the engine. He sprung from the car and ran for the front door. Minutes later cars roared away from the house towards the town. Both Nancy and the Wren climbed out of the car and began to run through the main corridor of the house towards Number 10. Downstairs the usual uniformed men and women sat across the top deck of Number 10. As she entered Nancy saw a frantic commotion with everyone either on the telephone or barking orders out. Those on the lower level were in a similar state of activity. She heard Sir's voice.

"Get your people out there now, including the medics, and find out what that dreadful stuff is."

"It's not mustard gas, Sir. If it was…"

"I know it's not mustard gas; just find out what it is."

He bent his head to cough again. "That roadblock," he said between fresh spasms, "are we assuming it was to steal or destroy the munitions from the factory?"

"That's right, Sir, and a right brazen plan as well, to literally steal it from under our noses."

"And did they?"

"No, Sir; we think we managed to get the message through before it moved off. The trucks are still sitting there now waiting for our command."

"Well keep them where they are," said Sir.

"London will want to know what is happening," piped up a Wren.

"They'll want to know a whole lot more if the whole lot is blown to kingdom come," replied Sir. He gazed down at the map before he looked up. He scanned the faces of those around him. "Where's Peach?" he said.

"Not here, Sir," said one of the young men in uniform.

"Well find him man!"

The young man saluted and ran from the room.

"How did they know the delivery was to be tonight?" barked Sir. "Only a handful at the factory and a few here knew. I simply don't understand it." He looked up towards the upper level. "Make sure that delivery is safe – and everything else besides. Put every man and woman you have on it to protect it: I don't care if it's the Girl Guides."

Once more telephones were raised and more orders relayed across the town.

THE BROCHURE

2010

Over the previous weeks Arthur had seen Mr Smith's various moods. He'd seen him irritated, tense, full of purpose and then full of regret. But it wasn't until he went back the following Saturday that he saw him angry. Even before he said anything Arthur could see the man's lips were clenched together into a firm line. He seemed to have more energy and walked strongly into the kitchen. Arthur's heart began to beat faster. "He knows, he knows," he said to himself over and over.

Mr Smith sat down but Arthur remained standing. He wanted to be able to bolt through the front door if the old man began shouting. But he didn't. He simply sat, looking at Arthur, his gaze fixed.

"I have to tell him," thought Arthur to himself. "Maybe that way he won't be so mad; he may understand." He went to open his mouth, but was stopped by Mr Smith's words, which came first.

"I'm a bit out of sorts today lad; had a visit, you see."

"What visit?"

Mr Smith reached across the table and grabbed hold of something. He lifted it up. It was a brochure with a photograph of a large manor house with open lawns and a large, sweeping drive. Arthur wanted to look closer but Mr Smith slammed it down again.

"Social services have been round, like they have a right," he said. "They want to farm me off to this place, an old people's home. I think someone's after my house, after the land anyway. What are they going to do: build a motorway? As if I ever could go to that place..." His voice trailed off.

Arthur reached for the brochure and held it up. "I know it, or at least I've seen it," he said. "It's Megg House, isn't it? I saw a photograph of it at the library the other day."

"They're so desperate that they're advertising there now are they? Trying to hook in the old dears as they return their books? The cheek of it. They've no idea what they're asking of me, well how could they, they've no idea about anything."

"No, no," said Arthur. "There's an exhibition there on the War, the Second World War, and there was a photograph of it. Someone said it had been involved in something secret during the War, they said..."

He was jolted by Mr Smith's raised voice. "I know what it was and I don't want to hear anymore about it," he said, his voice raised.

Arthur took a step towards him. He felt relieved at not being found out and it had made him bold. "No, you don't get it. They want people to tell them what it did during the War. They said it was so secret that not many people know."

As he said these words he watched Mr Smith get to his feet. Arthur continued: "You're old enough to remember the War: maybe you could tell them something.

Was that what the reporter was on about the other week?"

Mr Smith was crossing the small kitchen. He brushed past him and into the hallway. Arthur followed him into the living room. "What's wrong?" he asked. "I'm not saying I want you to go there; I'm just saying they want people to talk about it."

Mr Smith turned to him. "I said I don't want to hear anymore about it," his voice rising with each word. "Don't ever mention that place to me, ever, you understand?"

"I was only telling you."

"Well don't."

The old man slumped into a chair. Arthur didn't know what to do. After a while he went to sit on the sofa. He stared down at the filthy carpet. He was upset and his heart had begun to thump again, but after a minute or so it began to calm.

"I think the woman at the library even said something about German spies."

"Oh did she? Well, my father was German so maybe they want to accuse me of being one while I'm living there. They'll probably see that as some kind of justice."

Arthur looked across. "Your father was German?"

"As was half my family."

"Did he fight in the first War? Is that why you've got that old photograph…"

The words were out before he could stop them. Mr Smith looked up sharply. "What did you say?" he asked.

"Nothing, I just…"

"You just what? Tell me."

Arthur looked down. He felt ashamed of his own guilt.

"I saw some photographs here the other day, just a few, nothing much."

"Where, where did you see them?"

"In an old briefcase in the other room."

"You went in there without my permission?"

Arthur felt the tears prickling his eyes. "I only wanted to see what was in there; I didn't touch anything else. You have to believe me."

Mr Smith got up out of his chair. Before, he had always looked so frail, but now he seemed taller than Arthur ever remembered him, and strong as well. The man's raised voice made him jump again.

"I want you to leave and never come back," he said.

Arthur sprang to his feet and made for the hallway. He ran down it and reached for the lock, forcing it in his hand. Moments later he was running down the drive tears streaming down his face.

Arthur heard nothing from Mr Smith for many weeks. Luckily for him no-one at home questioned him about why his weekly visits had come to an end. After all, school had restarted and now he was trying to cope with a new timetable. The days grew shorter and soon the shops were filled with Christmas lights. He had tried to forget his old friend, telling himself that he wasn't important: he was just another silly old man.

December arrived, and with it the Christmas cards. One afternoon, after school, Arthur came home as usual and went to get something to eat when he saw an envelope propped up on the kitchen table. It was addressed to him. He opened it. It was a card showing snow and robins. The handwriting inside was so messy that he could hardly read it. "I'm sorry lad, I'm sorry," it read. It was from Mr Smith! He read on. "I know you want to know more and I have decided it is time. Will you come to see me? I have a story to tell you, and only you."

Underneath he'd been given a date and time. Arthur stuffed the card back in the envelope, smiled and went upstairs to hide it under his bed.

QUESTIONS AND A PLAN

1940

It was late when Nancy finally made it home, long after the dance must have finished. She hadn't wanted to leave Megg House but Sir had insisted. "Nothing more for you to do tonight and your parents will be worried," he had said, waving away her protests.

She was driven home. Father opened the door. "Oh love, love; where have you been, love?" he asked, throwing his arms around her.

Mother appeared behind him. "Where on earth? We've been going out of our minds. Mrs Drew said she saw you getting into a car."

Nancy drew back from Father's arms and looked between her parents. "It's nothing; I just got drawn into a bit of Guide work, that's all," she said.

Mother stared. "Don't give me that. We've been hearing that rubbish from you for months now. Just what is going on, girl?"

Nancy glanced up at her Father for support, but instead of calming her mother as he usually did in these moments, he too was looking at Nancy searchingly, asking for an answer. Nancy felt a stab of guilt and regret. "I've told you; now I'm tired, so I'm going to bed."

She walked through the living room and towards the staircase, Mother and Father following behind. They followed her up the stairs and into her room. Her mother was shouting again, pleading, imploring her to stop and explain. But Nancy couldn't explain to them any more than she could to herself. She had signed the Official Secrets Act, she was trying to rid the town of spies, and may even have stumbled upon a double-agent in the process, but how could she be sure?

She pulled off her thin party dress and opened the wardrobe. Mother was standing over her, Father in the doorway. "You speak to her," Mother said, turning to her husband.

"Look," shouted Nancy at last, "There's a War on, or haven't you noticed? I've been asked to help with the Guides, that's all. And no, I don't tell you everything about it, because I'm not supposed to."

Nancy had never raised her voice to her parents before and it was hard to tell who was the most shocked, them or herself. She threw herself into bed and pulled the covers over. She looked up at their faces. "I'm not in any trouble," she said quietly, "I promise you."

"This isn't over, young lady, and tomorrow morning I demand a proper explanation," said Mother, retreating into the hallway.

The house eventually went silent. Nancy slid out of bed and wandered over to Audrey's dressing table. She sat on the floor and leant against the thick, flowery material that cascaded down to the floor in soft folds. What was she to do? Every day she felt a panic rising from her growing feelings of betrayal towards her own family. She knew Father and Audrey were in danger up at Langleys; tonight confirmed it. They had made it through; everyone had made it through: but what about the next time? Every ear at Megg House was straining to intercept the spy ring, to catch them, especially the leader, the most dangerous spy of all, Sir had said. And then there was Peach. Was he a traitor, one of them or one of us? Nancy believed she was the only one not completely convinced of his loyalty to the Megg House cause, to the British cause. How could she do nothing? The threat hanging over Orethorpe was too great and the shadow of suspicion had already begun to draw itself around her own family.

She reached for some paper and began to write her account. It was a letter to her family, her confession about all she knew and her plea for forgiveness. But as she did so a word began to play back in front of her. The word was '*treason*'. It was treason to break the Official Secrets Act, so she tore up the paper into little pieces and began to write something else. This was no confession, this was a theory, her way of making sense of everything she had seen and heard. Putting it down on paper made it seem so simple, so obvious. Miss Temple was the ringleader, the one in charge of coordinating the spies. Peach was undoubtedly her mole at Megg House, diverting everyone away from the spy ring. Maybe he was even planting false intercepts or destroying true ones. Maybe he would warn them if the vans were getting close. He and Miss Temple had no doubt put a plan together, how to find out what each factory was producing and when it was to be dispatched. Their plan then was to starve the British of their supplies of arms by destroying or seizing them before they reached the front lines. At the same time they were bringing down morale with a blitz of bombing. It was to remind them, the British, who was coming, who was really in charge, and who was winning.

FOLLOWING PEACH

1940

Nancy did nothing. In truth, she didn't have much option for Mother and Father watched her every move. The day after the dance they had again demanded explanations. Once more, Nancy had tried to bluster her way through. Mother was unconvinced and even instructed Father to march up to Megg House to demand an explanation of what they were doing with his daughter. This threw Nancy into a minor panic but, when she had calmed down, she reflected with some amusement how Sir would respond. He would, no doubt, be charming and invite Father into his office, maybe even offer him a cup of tea. He'd smile while telling Father how useful the Guides had been in some mundane way; typing letters, making cups of tea for the staff at the house, taking the post. He would apologise for the secrecy. "Well, there's a War on and we're bound by our oaths not to breathe a word, mind you, all very silly when it comes to the trivial stuff of War that the Guides do," he would say, standing up and offering his hand, showing Father that the interview was over.

Father didn't go, at least he didn't appear to. For now, he seemed happy to have Nancy under the family roof, under his eye which is where she remained, or so he thought. But the following day Nancy rose early and dressed quickly. Mother and Father were still asleep. On entering the living room Nancy saw Mary sat at the table, bent over an array of pictures spread out in front of her.

"You're off earlier than usual, more Guide work I suppose," Mary looked up with a smile. Unlike Audrey she was always ready with a kind word for her younger sister.

"What are you looking at?" Nancy tried to divert the conversation.

"Hats, hats and more hats. Weddings eh? You having some breakfast?"

"In a bit, I have to pop out to run an errand."

"Okay, see you in a bit." Mary looked down again.

Nancy closed the front door quietly behind her. The street was virtually empty but she knew it would soon be filled with tired factory workers coming off their night shifts and reluctant ones going to start their daily toil.

Eventually she rounded the drive towards Megg House. The sun had barely risen and the buildings were draped in a low mist. It looked deserted. Nancy crouched behind a tree. She had now worked it all out. It must be the week of Peach's night shifts. If it was then he would go for a walk after the handover meeting, as she had seen him do many times. There was no reason to suppose he wouldn't take his usual route, out of the front door and down the drive.

The morning air was bitter and she silently prayed that she wouldn't have to wait too long. Her prayer was answered for, around ten minutes later, she saw the front door of Megg House open and a figure emerge. It didn't bother to follow the drive round but, instead, walked across the lawns. She flattened her back against the tree as she sensed it approach. The figure didn't stop but continued towards the road. Even from the back she recognised it. It was Peach.

She allowed him to disappear around the sharp bend leading to the road. Then she began to slowly walk after him. She didn't see him again until she reached the road. In front of her she saw his hat bobbing up and down as he descended the hill, towards town. She followed some distance behind.

It was another few minutes before Nancy realised they were heading towards the railway station. The station was once a red-roofed ticket office and waiting room and one platform sheltered by a tin roof. Just before the outbreak of the War it had been hastily extended, with platforms added and even a new line of track running to the Thorpe and Price factory. One advantage of these alterations was that one of the new platforms was in the open air and visible from the road. She watched as Peach entered the ticket office and emerged on the platform. His back was to her.

Nancy glanced over towards the platform. A wire fence separated it from the street. She turned back and took about thirty paces before darting right, down a grassy bank and towards the fence away from the station and platform. Wanting to see where the fence ended she walked along until she came to the wall of a half-derelict building. "Probably the original ticket office or something like that," she thought to herself. There didn't seem to be any way of getting through.

She kicked the bottom of the fence in frustration and as she did so the wire mesh suddenly flapped open. The gap was no more than a couple of feet at ground level, but it would be enough. Nancy crawled through. She quickly darted around the derelict building, making sure she couldn't be seen. It was then that she heard the slow chugging sound of a train on its approach. Here was another piece of luck for when it came to rest she could see that the last carriage was in front of her. It was empty and unlit. Without thinking, Nancy ran onto the platform and towards the carriage door. She pulled on the handle and the door flew open. She reached out and pulled the door shut, crouching on the floor, beneath the window.

There she stayed, breathing in the smell of musty furniture and stale air. Eventually the floor beneath her jolted and began to move. The lights of the station flashed across the carriage walls as the train gathered speed. Soon the engines had relaxed into an unhurried rhythm. Nancy uncurled herself and sat facing the seat opposite.

Before long the train began to slow. Eventually it creaked to a stop. She leant up to look out of the window. "We're in the middle of nowhere," she thought to herself. The front of the train was sat beside a tiny platform. All around were huge trees, their branches swaying in the strong wind. She heard a train door open. Allowing herself another glance Nancy saw Peach stepping onto the platform. He was alone. Just then the train began to move again.

Nancy pushed the carriage door open. Stretching out her arms she threw herself out of the carriage. Upon landing, the hard, cold ground seem to rock beneath her, but fortunately she had come to rest in some grass. The train was steaming and rumbling away and she saw that she was lying on a piece of barren land away from the platform. The light was still murky, but ahead she could see Peach standing beside the tiny station building. Nancy got onto her hands and knees and began to crawl towards the station.

She reached a spot within a few paces of the building and crouched down. It was then that she saw the small light bobbing down the track. It was coming from the opposite end of the platform. Peach must have seen it too for he walked several paces ahead. A man emerged from the gloom holding a torch in the early morning dawn. The pair exchanged words and began to walk down the platform, disappearing inside the tiny station building.

Nancy ducked down low and began crawling again. Soon she reached the concrete of the platform. A small window of the building above her head was open. She stretched up enough to put her head against the brickwork straining to hear. Inside the men were talking.

"It's been a long time."

"Yes, it has."

"Why now?"

"Isn't it obvious?"

"Not to me."

"Then maybe this will make it clear to you."

There was a rustling sound.

"Intercepts?"

"Yes, intercepts"

The voices were growing louder. There were more rustling sounds, like paper being screwed up.

"Oh I understand all right." The voice was louder.

"Do you?" came the reply.

"I've tried to protect you." That voice was Peach, she knew it for certain.

"Shut up, shut up, you know nothing about it," said the other man.

Feet were being stamped. Suddenly a pair of heavy boots thumped onto the platform. Nancy peered closer through the window into the room. The open door onto the platform only gave her a glimpse of the second man as he stood there.

"Do your job and I'll do mine," he shouted back at Peach, who remained in the room.

Peach did not move but a moment later the mysterious man was running, this time towards the spot where Nancy had jumped from the train. Peach began to shout at him from the platform. "And what job is that, eh, what job is that?"

The man swung around, his face briefly bathed in the light of the station platform, before he turned back again and began to run. Peach followed him, shouting again and again. Nancy watched as their ribbon-like forms quickly disappeared into the surrounding woodland. She was now all alone.

Some time passed and all remained quiet. Nancy pulled her coat around herself and began to walk. She thought there was a road, perhaps half a mile or a mile away and guessed that she was around two, maybe three miles, from the town. She decided however to follow the train track back to Orethorpe. The walk was hard work but it warmed her body and, after several minutes, began to clear her mind. The fear of discovery had passed and had been replaced with a renewed sense of righteousness. She had been right about Peach all along. She had been right, and Tom had been wrong. Sir had been wrong to trust him, as had all the others. She had been right, she alone had been right!

The line of the train track came towards an expanse of open fields. During the summer months the churned soil would have squelched and splashed up to her socks and onto her skin. Today it was as bronze, frozen into ruts as hard as the iron train tracks she was following. Her feelings of righteousness turned to something else: the sense of betrayal. Peach had been pretending to be one of them. He had mirrored their thoughts, echoed their words and repeated their own actions, even directed them. But the truth was truly terrible. He was not drawing the poison from the town, he was injecting it.

The train track submerged into a short, blackened tunnel before it emerged in front of the Old Toll House. With relief, Nancy understood that she was nearing the town. This relief seemed to release more recollections and her thoughts switched to the second man. Had she seen him before? She suddenly stopped. Yes! Yes, she had! She replayed those few seconds on the platform over in her mind. The answer was some minutes coming, but when the truth broke free from her memory it was enough to jolt her entire body. She *had* seen him before. The first time he had been wearing smart civilian clothes inside the café, leaning against the counter, ordering drinks for himself and Miss Temple. The second time he had ducked and skipped as the bullets whirled and spat around his feet at Graves End Wood!

CONFRONTING PEACH

1940

Peach was a spy. He was a double-agent, a traitor and an enemy of everything they stood for and were trying to protect. He had been seen driving off with Miss Temple, probably to meet with his other spy friends, and had now met up with the spy from the wood: but to do what? Punish him for almost getting caught and putting the whole mission in danger?

Entering Number 10 the next day, Nancy had just one aim in mind – to find Sir and tell him everything. She found him standing beside the map. She felt enormously relieved, but then she noticed the others by his side. They were much older, they wore more colours on the breasts of their uniforms and had sterner expressions. Her heart sank when she saw someone else standing on the edge of the group. It was Peach.

Nancy went up to one of the Wrens. "Who are those men?" she asked.

"'Top brass' up from London," replied the woman.

"Why?"

"They're not happy with how things are being handled."

Sir turned to face her. "Ah, Miss Brown, just the person. I've been telling the Group Captain here about our adventure the other night."

Nancy was avoiding Peach's eyes but he then rounded the table and came and stood beside her. "Let's not jump to conclusions at that," said Peach, his voice calm and controlled to diffuse suspicion, so unlike the last time she had heard it.

He turned back to a Wren to say something and then twisted to face Nancy again.

Suddenly, it was all too much for Nancy to bear and she ran at him, flung herself on his chest and began to pummel her fists into him.

"Who are you? Who are you?" she cried aloud.

He had grabbed her flailing arms and tried to push her away. She fought to wrestle free and pulled the trunk of her body away from him, shouting again as she did so. Suddenly he released her, sending her body careering backwards. She landed on the floor.

"Go and calm yourself down," he shouted, walking up to her, grabbing her by the arm and forcing her to her feet. "Any more of that and it won't be your parents I'll be calling, it will be the police."

She shook him away and stepped backwards. They stared at each other. The pretend friendship was over and now they faced each other as enemies, for Nancy was certain that is what they were. The voices on the upper level had grown quiet. Everywhere faces stared down at them.

"Someone, take her upstairs to my room," shouted Sir. The command was not directed at any one person and everyone simply stood or sat where they were.

"That's an order!" Sir shouted again. Still no-one moved and Nancy felt her courage rise once again.

"You have a lot of explaining to do, a lot of questions to answer," she bellowed.

"You're overwrought," said Peach. "Now is someone going to get her out of here?"

One of the young men walked over and put his arm around her. "He's right," he whispered in Nancy's ear. "You're overstressed that's all." He led her up the stairs and out of the room. It wasn't long before the sound of voices and telephones resumed in Number 10.

She waited inside Sir's office. Eventually he entered, but he was not alone: the 'top brass' accompanied him. Ignoring the others, Nancy rushed to him as soon as the door opened.

"Peach is a spy, he's a spy I tell you," she cried out. "I saw him talking to Miss Temple and yesterday he was with the man, Miss Temple's friend, the man from the woods on the night of the explosion. You remember? They were at a train station and they were talking about intercepts and protecting the spies. You have to believe me, you have to, you have to."

Sir stepped away from her and towards his desk. He looked embarrassed by her behaviour and looked across towards his superiors. "Peach is a spy, you say?"

"Yes, I saw him talking to the man in the woods. I saw him that night of the explosion. Last night I saw them together. I tell you, they were together."

"Where was this?"

"On a station platform. I followed Peach there." She relayed her story of the spy ring, the trip to Station X and her adventures on the train, seeing Peach meet the mysterious man, the one she'd seen before. It was all so obvious, why wouldn't they believe her?

"I'll question him about it," said Sir when she had finished.

One of the 'top brass' stepped forward. "This is ridiculous, Wing Commander. She's nothing but a girl. What are you doing, using children: what are you running here?"

Sir looked over towards him. "She's one of our best interceptors."

"Poppycock," said one of the other men. "I wager you'll find nothing. She's delusional."

"Nancy, wait outside, would you?" asked Sir.

She retreated into the hallway and sat down on a hard chair facing the office. Inside she could hear raised voices. After several minutes the 'top brass' emerged. Sir was behind them. "In here, Miss Brown," he said. She re-entered the office and sat down.

"You're relieved of duties." He raised his hand when she went to protest. "It's just for now, until we sort this out, understood? Those men are not happy and they can shut us down in a moment, and they insist on this. Just stay away for a while, until I say so. Wait until you hear from me."

"But he's a spy, Sir, I saw him, I heard him. What if they bomb the factory tonight or tomorrow and you and I could have prevented it?"

"I'll have him questioned about it: in fact, I'll do it myself. But these are extremely serious accusations, you realise that? As for you, well I need to keep you and Peach apart for the time being, that's for certain."

Nancy went to protest but he raised his hand again to silence her. "It's just for now, Nancy, just for now and orders are orders."

GOING BACK

2010

Arthur didn't have to knock on the door, for Mr Smith was waiting for him. He stood in the hallway, holding his hat and a new stick.

"Where are we going?" asked Arthur. "I've brought money for the bus..." Mr Smith raised his hand to silence him.

"We don't need the bus today, boy," he said. He smiled. "We're not going far."

Outside, Mr Smith groped around in his pocket for his keys. With a shaking hand he locked the door and held out his arm for Arthur's support. The pair began to walk slowly down the drive.

"I owe you an apology, dear friend," said Mr Smith. "I should never have reacted like that. Can you forgive me?"

"Yes, of course." The apology made Arthur feel embarrassed and he wanted to talk about something else. "Where are we going?" he asked again, but there was no reply.

They walked for several minutes until, eventually, Mr Smith tugged on Arthur's arm to turn left, away from the main road. They walked up a narrow, pot-holed road that Arthur knew led to a row of expensive houses overlooking the valley of Orethorpe. He began to wonder if they were to take in the view of the town while Mr Smith mused some more on days past, so it was a surprise when the old man leant on his arm to indicate they were to turn into the sweeping driveway to the right. It led to what looked like an old hotel, but was in fact the old people's home, the brochure for which had previously so upset Mr Smith. "I wonder if he's planning to move in here after all," Arthur thought to himself.

The drive up to the large house was sloping, and Mr Smith leant heavily on his stick and then on Arthur until they got to the top. The old man breathed deeply in and out, but didn't stop. Neither did he speak again until they were ascending the stone steps and through an invitingly open door. "Now, that's better," he said, stopping in front of a mirror. The hallway had oak-panelled walls and a heavily patterned carpet. The sound of shouting could be heard from one of the rooms, together with the clang of saucepans. Cutlery was being banged onto tables in the room nearest them. Someone down the hall was playing the piano over a loud chatter. They walked up the corridor towards the noisy room. They paused at the door, looked in, and saw that it was full of people. They were all packed in together, standing in what space they could find in the large, rectangular room. Glancing around, Arthur noticed how old many of the people were. He saw that the women wore long, pleated skirts worn together with flat shoes. Their hands held glasses of champagne and orange juice. The men wore suits and smart navy blazers against loose, khaki trousers. Almost all of them wore medals on their jackets.

There were some of a younger generation as well, even though they still looked older than Arthur's mother. Many were laughing loudly. Some would hold out their hand to one of the older people, or occasionally give them a pat on one shoulder. One middle-aged man wore a large, gold chain around his tweed jacket. He was bent over an invalid woman in a wheelchair, talking loudly. Mr Smith held out his hand. Arthur took it and stepped into the room. Arthur found a small opening in the crowd to the right and began to guide Mr Smith through it. As they made their way around the room they had to step over several out-stretched feet and walking sticks. Reaching a wall they saw that a little stage had been put up. Above it was a banner with the words, *MEGG HOUSE REUNION 1939-1941.*

Mr Smith stood leaning on his stick, his face tipped upright, his eyes covering the room. A young waitress, no more than nineteen years old, approached holding a metal tray. Someone had arranged tiny pancakes smeared with some kind of paste. She held out the tray to them but Mr Smith simply shook his head. Arthur took one of the delicacies and popped it in his mouth. It had a strong, fishy taste he didn't like. He looked over towards Mr Smith again. The old man's eyes looked moistened. They had lost that distant look, the one that told Arthur that the man was thinking of something else, someone else, far away or long lost. Now his gaze was as intent as Arthur had ever seen it. They remained there, almost motionless, for more than twenty minutes. Arthur had never known Mr Smith to remain standing for so long and eventually motioned that he was going to find him a chair. Mr Smith broke his gaze to look back at him. "Thank you, son, but there's no need for that," he said. "But I would like some air."

They began picking their way once again through the crowd. Mr Smith directed them to a large open bay window. The adjoining wall was panelled with a rich-coloured wood and had a stone fireplace. Mr Smith put his back to the wall, rested and looked across the room. He nudged Arthur and the boy looked around.

"We're not leaving just yet, follow me," said Mr Smith as he began to edge slowly along the wall.

"What is all this about?" asked Arthur, following. "What's the reunion for?"

"A reunion for those who served in the War, of course: what else?" said Mr Smith.

"But why here?" asked Arthur.

Mr Smith turned to face him. "Not all the fighting was done abroad, you know, laddie," he said. "Some of it took place here, in a way. This is Megg House remember."

Mr Smith edged into an alcove in the wall which reached from floor to ceiling. He stepped into it and took a step to the left. Within a second he was obscured from view. He reached out his hand to touch a section of wood panelling. He pushed hard and the next moment a section moved. Mr Smith pushed again, and as he did so the entire section of wall moved. It was some kind of door leading into total darkness. Mr Smith stepped through.

"Where are you going? What's in here?"

"The past, my boy, the past." Mr Smith was sliding his hand down the wall by the inside door frame.

"It's here, I can feel it the light switch, ah that's it," he said.

Arthur leant back. "What are you doing?" he said. "If anyone finds us we'll be shot."

To his surprise the old man simply chuckled. "Not anymore, we won't. Those days are long gone. Give over, now; come on." Suddenly Arthur heard a soft click and to his amazement the cavity inside the wall was bathed in light. A puff of dust and mouldy air rose up, making the old man cough.

"We can't do this," Arthur said.

"I'll answer for it, I promise you," said Mr Smith. "I'm too old to worry about trouble now: I've seen enough of the real stuff in my time. Folk today have no idea what trouble is. Now, are you coming or not? Quick, before people see us."

Arthur studied his face for a few moments. Even at his tender age he could sense absolute determination in the way the creases around the man's eyes had frozen as he gazed at him. The man's mouth had locked in a fixed line. The boy nodded.

Two rapid steps took him through the door which Mr Smith firmly closed. Below him he could see a stone stairway reaching down.

"Go down; go down, and I'll follow you," said Mr Smith, shuffling to let him past.

Arthur descended the icy-cold steps, counting ten until the bottom. He turned to see Mr Smith's shaky legs and his thin, veined hands clutching a metal handrail. Arthur held out his hand to his friend and helped him down the last two steps. They stood there facing each other.

They were in a corridor with grimy whitewashed walls and a high ceiling lit by a single bulb. Great clumps of mould had gathered in the corners. Spiders had made great sport, for huge webs were draped between the walls like a housewife's washing on the line. The air was freezing and thick, with a funny smell of what, exactly, Arthur couldn't tell. But when he turned to Mr Smith he saw a pair of old eyes fixed on the line of the corridor in front of them.

"Listen," said Arthur, "I've had enough and I want to go home."

Mr Smith said nothing, but remained fixed on the line of brickwork leading away.

"We shouldn't be down here," Arthur continued; "we're going to be caught."

Still Mr Smith said nothing. Instead, he began to slowly plod his way down the corridor, in the direction of his steady gaze. He continued further down towards the dimness where the single bulb couldn't reach. He was about to step into the gloom when he put his hand to something on his right. The next moment the entire corridor was flooded with the light of a dozen bulbs.

"I thought so," said Mr Smith, looking back towards Arthur. "I was hoping they'd work."

"How do you know about this place?" asked Arthur. But the old man wasn't listening. He was walking, walking down the newly-lit corridor.

They passed several doors, all shut, until they came upon a set of double-doors. Something had been painted on them, some letters, but Arthur could not make them out.

Mr Smith turned and said: "Arthur my dear, dear friend, can you open them for me?" His voice was suddenly weak and trembling. "I know it's one of these," he mumbled to himself.

For a moment Arthur's curiosity had overcome his fear and, without complaining, he shoved himself against the doors. They opened easily, almost sending him falling forward into the unknown.

"That's it," said Mr Smith as he held the double doors open. Together they shuffled through and the old man went over to a wall to the right and flicked a switch. A set of lights sprung on, sending a yellow hue over the large room before them.

They stood at the top of an upper tier. It housed a row of solid, wooden desks. There chairs had been pushed back, some lying on top of each other, others on their sides. A layer of thick, dense dust the colour of grey slate covered the desks' surface, turning what looked like tin mugs, packets, files, pens, briefcases and boxes into mounds of dirty sand on a desert plain. Within the mess Arthur could see the shapes of several large old-fashioned telephones in a row.

Ahead of them was the lower level. A huge table dominated the room. One of its legs had given way and it had buckled to the right. A curtain of grey-coloured paper could be seen strewn across it and dribbling onto the floor. It looked like the remnants of an old map of Orethorpe. Dust and papers were everywhere. They covered the floor and stairs, some were piled on yet more desks and some were even pinned across the walls. To Arthur it seemed as though this was the scene of some great crime, which, when the deed was done, had been abandoned and hastily sealed for all eternity. Whatever happened here, no-one had had the stomach or the desire to sweep the floors, straighten the furniture or tidy away the files.

Arthur looked across to Mr Smith who stared forward then held out his hand for his young friend to take.

"Well blow me, blow me," said Mr Smith; then, again, "Blow me, after all this time, after all this time."

"You know this place then?" asked Arthur.

"I've never been here before in my life," said Mr Smith.

"Then how did you know it was here?"

"I was briefed boy, I was briefed. It was my job to know it was here, to know the layout, the work being done in the different rooms, even who was doing it. Night after night I studied the plans to this place, even the photographs. I had to know what was happening here, but to see it now, to see it now..."

His voice trailed off and he motioned for Arthur to help him. He began shuffling his feet towards the stairs, rustling the loose papers at his feet. Arthur helped him down the short staircase and into the main body of the room. Mr Smith did not stop to inspect the table or bother to look over the items left on the desks. Instead, he continued shuffling his way across to one of the walls. He went up to it and put out his hand for Arthur to steady him. He reached up with his other hand and began to brush away the dust with his sleeve. Arthur looked closer. As the old man brushed away he could see what looked like a board underneath. Mr Smith began to mumble. "Damn and blast, all that death and destruction by them."

"Who?" asked Arthur.

"The Germans and their spies of course."

"What spies?"

The old man didn't answer but continued brushing away at the board. Suddenly they heard a door slam. Arthur swung round. Someone was standing in the doorway to the room. He was old and thin. He was staring at Mr Smith who turned to look at the intruder. The mysterious man took a step forward and raised his hand.

"I knew it!" he said, his tone angry. "I knew you'd come."

A MISERABLE CHRISTMAS

1940

Nancy did not hear from Megg House following her dismissal. Christmas morning arrived. She stood next to Father in church as he choked out the words to some carol. Afterwards the family slid back over the snow and ice towards home.

Modest presents were opened followed by Christmas lunch, a thin affair of rabbit stew and boiled potatoes followed by a strange pudding mix made up of wartime mincemeat and carrot fudge. The five of them sat around the table talking about the bitter cold of the church that morning, the strange hat worn by the organist's wife and what would be on the wireless that night.

Afterwards Nancy and Mary had retreated to Joyce's, in search of some cheer, but even there the laughter sounded a little too forced and the chatter would often fall to silence. Kep was there but his gentle ways were not enough to lift more than an occasional smile from his own parents. It was not even 5 o'clock when he got up to leave, telling them he was expected back at the RAF station. His mother reached up to give her eldest son a hug. She kissed him twice on the cheek, held him for several moments more than usual and put her hand on his sleeve.

"Mind how you go, pet," she said.

"Yes, Mother," he said softly.

Mr Harris drew himself up from his armchair by the fire and held out his hand. "I don't know why you have to go, today of all days, and I don't want to know, but you be careful," he said.

"I will, Dad," said Kep.

The next moment he was gone, his coat draped over his arm. Mrs Harris turned back to the fire. "He'll catch his death, he will; how many times do I have to tell him to wear his coat?" she said. She began clearing away the tea things. Nancy saw her draw her sleeve across her eyes.

"The young don't feel it as bad as we do, Mabel," said Mr Harris. Nancy wondered if he was referring to the weather or the hardship and dangers of the War.

LOW FLYING

1940

It was New Year before Nancy managed to leave the house on her own. She had gone for an afternoon walk, promising herself that she would not venture up the hill towards Megg House. Instead she wandered around the back streets circling the square. Before she knew it she was at the top of Diver's Hill on the edge of town, almost half a mile away from the central square. It was nearly dusk before she swung round to head home. She did not know this side of Orethorpe as well as other parts. The gas lamps in the street would not be coming on as they had before the War and she would have to hurry if she was not to risk getting lost. She began to jog and skip down the hill, the dark shadows chasing her along the icy pavements. She rounded a corner and, without looking, ran into the solid column of an older man. Before she knew it he had enclosed his arms around her.

"Well I'm pleased to see you too," he joked. It was Mr Harris, Joyce's father. "Do your folks know you're out at this hour?"

"No, yes, well, kind of, but I'm on my way back." She stumbled out the words.

"I'll walk you; that way I'll know you'll get back safe."

"No, no, really, it's very kind but I can walk faster than you and you're going the other way."

"Nonsense, I can't go back to the Missus and tell her I let you walk home on your own, she wouldn't have it."

They were just making their way towards town when they heard them. The aeroplanes hummed as they approached the town. "What the devil?" said Mr Harris, staring skywards. There was nothing to be seen. "Why the deuce don't they sound the air raid sirens?" He looked around him. "Come on: the nearest shelter is up the road," he said. "We'll have to make a run for it. It's..."

His voice was suddenly drowned out by the lion's roar of a large, black form which came into view above them. It was low, so low that it skipped and skimmed over the roofs and chimneys of the houses like the hull of a huge boat coming into shore. Mr Harris instinctively ducked. Nancy followed. The plane appeared to dip downwards as if it was about to attempt to land or do the unthinkable and crash directly into the central square. But, as they watched, the nose rose again and it swept over the opposite line of buildings, roaring into the distance.

"Did you see that?" cried Mr Harris. "Did you see it, it's one of ours."

An air raid warden standing nearby, shouted over to them. "It's blackout flying practice, it's got to be," he called out. "There's no way anyone would mistake that for the Luftwaffe; it's RAF for certain. We should know, we've seen them fly over enough."

Just then a second plane came into view over All Saints' Church. "Here comes another!" the warden shouted over to them. It followed the same pattern as the first, ducking slightly over the square before sweeping up into the black sky.

The warden was walking towards them. "I heard something about this from my mother in Dumbleton," he said to Mr Harris. "Some form of special training she was saying."

Mr Harris now looked embarrassed by his earlier outburst. He began leading Nancy away, across the square towards Pratts Lane and the maze of tiny streets beyond, which would eventually lead them out onto Abbots Road. He was mumbling something under his breath but Nancy could only catch odd words such as 'idiots' and 'shot down'. The centuries-old cobbles took them halfway across the square before the ground flattened out into a more modern road surface, suitable for market sellers, ladies with prams and the endless traffic of industry. Night-time and the blackout had turned the shops into shadowy, arched, gingerbread forms against a treacle sky, so the explosive interruption of lights made her and Mr Harris jolt forwards and stop once more. They looked upwards. Two massive lights could be seen moving and swaying over the night sky. Nancy instantly knew that they were anti-aircraft lights used during a German raid.

The next moment a plane swept overhead again, but this time flying away from them in the opposite direction to before. Nancy and Mr Harris watched it until it was swallowed up by the abyss of the midwinter night. But moments later it was caught up in one of the beams of light from the ground. They saw the plane duck, taking it out of view once more. It was then that they heard it, the sound of the anti-aircraft gun splattering into the sky. The light dipped and then there came the sound of more shells across the expanse of space. This time they didn't disappear into the air; they locked onto their target, the metal-on-metal contact sending a spark to the plane's core, shattering the fuselage and igniting the gas, leather and rubber within it. The plane, now a mass of flames, began to dive, its death-drone screaming out as it plunged towards the town. Nancy felt the ground beneath her shudder as the plane crashed before exploding. She couldn't breathe. The gigantic roar of impact deafened her ears. She tried to clamp them with her hands; she squeezed her eyes shut and buckled over. To her it seemed a very long time before she was aware of the hand tugging on her coat or the voice pleading with her to get up. She realized that she was crouched on her knees with her face almost bent to the ground.

"Get up; get up, we have to get out of here!" Mr Harris was shouting at her.

"I can't, I can't," Nancy shouted back.

"You have to! What if they bring one of those things down on our heads?" he shouted again.

"They've got the wrong one, the wrong one," she shouted back, still on her knees.

He was tugging at her arm again. "It's not safe here," he said. "Oh please get up, get up." He bent down, placed one of his arms under one of her elbows and forced her to her feet. Shock was etched across his face.

"Why, why did they do it?" Nancy cried.

"It's got to have been a mistake," he said. "Now come on." He was tugging at her sleeve again, leading her out of the exposed expanse of the square. They found themselves at Pratts clothing store on the corner.

THE MOST DANGEROUS SPY

Nancy flattened her back against the display window, taking in gulps of air.

"Can you run?" Mr Harris shouted again.

"Wait, wait," said Nancy.

"No, we can't wait," he yelled. "The nearest shelter is up there." He was pointing towards Tanners Lane leading off from the square.

"You don't think there's going to be any more?" cried Nancy.

"I don't know, but we must take shelter until we know it's safe. Come on," he pleaded.

They began to run. Nancy's legs were shaky and she was slow, too slow. She slipped across the ground and dropped into a walk. Ahead of them she could see red and orange rising up into the air. As they rounded the corner, the entrance to the shelter near Bewseys shop came into view. But so did something else. Cars and vans were racing towards them. They broke hard outside Bewseys and Nancy saw men in various uniforms push open the doors and hurl themselves out. All began racing towards the gap between two shops on the opposite side of the road. Nancy knew it led up to the rugby fields which had been fenced and gated off since the start of the War.

Mr Harris reached the shelter before her. When she arrived he waved his arms about, frantically guiding her down the stone stairs. Nancy obeyed and it wasn't until they were seated at the entrance to this place of safety that she turned to him.

"Did you see all those men?" she said while panting for breath. Mr Harris was also breathing heavily. Inside the shelter he removed his hat and wiped his forehead with his sleeve but kept looking towards the ground and didn't even look up when he answered her.

"I don't know what's going on," he said, still gulping for air. "They were headin' up towards one of the anti-aircraft bases. Might have been the one that shot down the poor blighters in that plane." He wiped his forehead again. "It's so bad, so bad, so bad," he said. He continued staring at the ground, only looking up to watch a young couple enter and sit down opposite them. The woman was shaking and the man was trying to soothe her. The warden in charge came thumping down the stairs. He was heavy and had a red nose and a kind face.

"Anybody hurt?" asked the warden in a raised voice. They were the only people inside. Most people stayed indoors during the blackouts. The young man looked up.

"We're all right, but did you see it?" he cried.

"I think we all did," said the warden, glancing around. He stepped further in. "There's a load of fellows descending on the anti-aircraft guns over yonder. I heard gunfire and dipped down here out of the way."

"What?" The young man was on his feet now. "Have we been invaded then?" he shouted. "It's come at last has it?" He began to move towards the exit but was stopped by the warden, who began shouting at him to sit down.

"We don't know what's happened yet, but if it was *that* we'd know about it for sure," said the warden.

He opened his mouth to say something else but at the very same moment came the sound of a fresh explosion. The fortified walls of the underground shelter dulled the jolting thud of the blast, but Nancy still felt the walls and floor shudder.

"What's going on now?" shouted the young man. The woman at his side began to whimper.

"Could be another plane's come down; I just don't know!" the warden shouted back.

"Well, go and find out, man!" yelled the young man.

The warden hesitated. He looked afraid, but was soon thumping up the stairs as fast as his fat, stubby legs would take him. The air became still as they waited. Mr Harris reached out to take Nancy under his arm.

"Never mind, love; we're safe, that's the main thing," he said in a quiet, soothing voice. "We'll soon get you home, eh?" He continued soothing her, unaware that she neither cried nor shook with fear. Earlier, in the square, she had been terrified by the awful scene of destructive death in front of her but now the shock was beginning to subside.

Several times more the warden poked his head around the entrance, warning them not to attempt escape. "I've got my orders now," he said, rather self-importantly. "You're to stay here until I say so, got that?" He disappeared back up the stairs again before anyone could reply.

Nancy thought it must have been close to dawn when release finally came, so was surprised to see the still black sky. The scene above ground was one of cars and vans crammed onto the road and pavements, shouting voices and a warm wind filled with ashes and an acrid, metallic stench.

"What on earth happened here?" said Mr Harris under his breath. He turned and was just about to speak to the warden when another voice came bellowing from across the road.

"Miss Brown!" She looked across to see Sir standing beside a wagon. His hands were in the pockets of his overcoat. He shouted again: "Miss Brown, over here!"

Mr Harris turned to her. "What does he want?" he said. "How does he know your name?"

Nancy didn't answer. She was walking across the road, weaving through the vehicles and coughing in the thick air. When she reached Sir she became aware that Mr Harris had followed her. "What do you want with her?" he asked.

"She can help us with something," replied Sir. Outwardly he remained calm, but Nancy could see streaks of tension etched across his face.

"What with? She's just a girl," said Mr Harris, sounding every inch the protective father.

"Miss Brown has helped us before with a matter of identification," said Sir. "I am hoping she can do so again. Now if I might ask you to move to the side, Sir, this is between Miss Brown and myself."

Mr Harris opened his mouth to protest but found himself being ushered off the scene and further down the street.

"What happened, what happened?" asked Nancy. "Please tell me, please. Did they shoot down the wrong plane? We saw it: it wasn't German, it was one of ours."

"I know that," said Sir. "But this was no accident."

He stepped aside and gestured for her to walk up the passageway between the shops. He followed behind. They emerged into a field around which a tall, metal fence had been erected. Sir motioned for a guard to let them through a gate. Once on the other side, Nancy saw around a dozen Auxiliary Fire Service personnel, some holding fire hoses, hosing down a great mound of metal. Sir stepped up to stand beside her.

"An anti-aircraft gun: supposed to protect us, then turned against us," he said. "They got hold of it, the spies. They ambushed the operators and got their hands on the guns themselves." He gestured towards a small, concrete bunker nearby. "Thankfully, our men turned up quicker than they thought and we managed to get two of them while they were escaping."

Two pairs of men, each carrying a stretcher, were coming across the field towards the gate. Sir gestured for them to stop. He walked Nancy over. One held a man, the other a woman. Without warning Sir reached over to one of the stretchers and gestured for Nancy to follow. There, laid on the stretcher, was a young woman, her face thin, her hair brown. Her hair was matted with blood and she was groaning. Nancy glanced down at her, but only for a moment, for Sir suddenly pulled her away and gave the men the order to go on. Without speaking, he walked her back to Tanners Road and motioned for her to get into a car. "You're coming back with us for now," said Sir once they were inside. He waved his hand at the driver as an order to depart.

They drove along in silence, up towards Megg House. The woman's face danced in front of Nancy's eyes, but she was in shock and it wasn't until they were crawling their way up the gravel drive of the house that the face came to her again; not lying on a stretcher, but in a street not even a mile away. She was the woman standing in the street with the other man arguing with Peach about the War Office leaflets. Then she had worn a hat with a protruding feather. Nancy had only just realised it but it suddenly came upon her that she had seen the woman a second time, at the roadblock. That time she had been in a coarse, plain uniform, holding a rifle. She had sworn and run away into the misty, smoky night after the mystery car had smashed its way through. Nancy had failed to put the two sightings together, until now.

The car pulled up outside the front door. Sir sprung out and opened the door for her. Leaping out, she turned to him. "I know who she is," she said.

"Do you?" he replied. "Well, so do we."

BACK TO NUMBER 10

1940

"Come with me," said Sir. He ran up the stairs and into the house, crossed the hall and entered the Intercept Room. Nancy followed him and was surprised to find only a single Wren. The woman was on the phone but put her hand over the mouthpiece when she saw Sir enter. "They're all downstairs, Sir," she said.

"How many anti-aircraft stations were taken?" asked Sir.

"Three that we know of, Sir," replied the Wren.

They made their way down to Number 10. The corridors below ground were thick with the bustle of several dozen men and women in various uniforms running from room to room. Upon seeing Sir coming towards them several tried to catch his eye or flag him down, but he brushed on past, barely even acknowledging them. A man in uniform met them outside Number 10. "We think the spies have taken control of the anti-aircraft guns, Sir, or destroyed them," he said.

"I know that, man, I know that," barked Sir.

"They were shooting down the RAF planes during blackout flying practice. But we've managed to fight back. Some of those who took control of the guns have been taken, arrested." He handed Sir a piece of paper.

Inside Number 10, Nancy could see five or six women were crowded around the central map, each wearing a set of headphones. More young men were standing around the boards to the side. Sir just waved the assembly back to work before he walked over to the boards.

"What can you tell me about the spies that have been arrested?" he addressed anyone who would listen.

A young man stepped forward. "Two men and one woman. Two had seized control of the guns near the town square, but you've just come from there haven't you, Sir? They used them then smashed the guns up. They were young and match the descriptions of a couple acting suspiciously a few weeks ago but we never managed to track them down. A third, older man was shot and wounded at the guns up near Jermyn Street. The guns there were also badly damaged. We don't yet know who he is. A second person with him managed to shoot his way out and escape."

Sir sighed deeply. "Two anti-aircraft stations destroyed," he said. "What of the others?"

The young man turned back to the map. "The anti-aircraft gun up on Bank wasn't used on the RAF. Apparently they tried to destroy it, but something must have gone wrong," he said. "We've got people on the way to the fourth."

Sir looked up and over towards the men and women manning the telephones on the upper level. "Did you hear that?" he bellowed. "Two anti-aircraft stations destroyed." All, except one very thin, lined man who was speaking on the telephone, looked down towards the group. They looked puzzled, even shocked. Sir continued. "One of you had better be ready with a good explanation as to why you weren't onto this faster when the Ministry comes asking," he shouted. "That's two guns down and three spies captured."

The young man spoke again: "Unfortunately they're badly hurt and will probably die of their injuries," he said. "Either way, we have a long wait before we can question them. So, right at this moment we're just as much in the dark as before."

One of the men stood up to answer back, but Sir ordered him to sit down. The man obeyed but began mumbling to the woman beside him. Sir had begun to pace backwards and forwards, backwards and forwards. He had always been so calm before, now the sight of him on the edge of panic made Nancy terribly afraid. The others stood aside watching. Sir continued pacing but then suddenly stopped. "Why risk capture or even death just to pick off a few RAF planes?" he said to no-one in particular. "It doesn't make sense. Langleys got its delivery out days ago. Tell me, why would they do this?"

There was silence before one of the younger men spoke up. "Perhaps if we know how they found out about the blackout flying it might give us a clue," he said. "Can't we question them straight away?"

"No, they are too badly injured and, anyway, we're not authorized," said Sir. "We'll have to wait for London to send someone, if any of them live that long."

There was a long pause which no-one seemed keen to fill. Just then one of the Wrens wearing headphones looked up. "Report coming in from the fourth station, Sir," she said. "The station is safe. No apparent attempt at sabotage. All field staff accounted for."

"Why target three and not all of them?" someone asked.

"Perhaps they didn't have the manpower," said Sir. "It's the spies, the very same people we've been tracking for months, make no mistake about that. Maybe we were getting too close and they were pressurized to do something, to make something of a show." He began pacing again, but just then the floor walker put down the telephone and stood up.

"Sir, Sir," he said. Sir looked up and nodded for the man to speak. "The Intercept Room has picked up something, Sir. They're bringing it over now."

"Did they say what it is?" asked Sir.

"An intercept from a spy; they're almost certain, they say," replied the man.

Several minutes later a young Wren ran through the door and down the stairs. She handed a small, brown piece of paper to the duty supervisor. He read it and handed it to Sir. "Just one word, Sir: BULLSEYE," he said.

"It didn't come through just once, but several times," said the Wren. "It wasn't even encrypted."

"So it was sent in a panic or they've feeling very confident?" asked Sir. "You know what it means?" he continued, holding the piece of paper aloft before the entire room. "Anyone? Come on, people, didn't you learn anything upstairs?"

"BULLSEYE: it's the code-word for night-time training runs during the blackout, Sir," said one of the men in uniform.

"Exactly," said Sir. "Whoever messaged this knew the RAF would be flying over us tonight. They knew it and they decided to do something about it. No wonder they were confident."

"But how did they know, Sir?" asked the Wren.

"Well, isn't it obvious," Sir asked. "Someone told them."

Sir looked at Nancy as he said these words. His mouth was twisted with worry and even pain. "Maybe now he believes me," she thought.

Just then a bright red light next to the clock began to glow. The Wrens, who had put down their wooden plotting sticks and loosened their headphones, jumped back into position around the map, covering their ears. One of them, the lead plotter on that shift, soon spoke. "Unidentified aircraft approaching the coast, Sir," she said.

She leant over the map and, using her stick, pushed a small, metal stand out to the far right edge of it. Sir was now accompanied by Peach, who had suddenly appeared, and, to Nancy's eyes, was looking suspiciously relaxed in all the confusion. Together they walked over to the map.

"They're coming in fast, Sir," said the lead plotter after several minutes. "At least four of them, same height as before." She placed several more stands onto the map.

The duty supervisor went over to her. "What grid reference?" he asked.

"Nothing definite yet," she answered. "They might not be heading our way. Wait, there's something else coming in now." She looked up. "They've reached land, Sir."

"Are they scrambling?" Sir bellowed down. Everyone knew he was referring to the RAF station not a mile away from Megg House. Nancy knew they would be receiving the same information and had to act fast. "But how can they if our fighters have just been shot down?" she thought to herself.

Several very tense minutes passed. The other plotters had also begun to receive information from the various military sectors ordered to filter information through to them. The aircraft were definitely hostile. At least four planes. High altitude. Coming over fast from the east. RAF scrambling what they have left.

The Sector Chiefs had already begun to make phone call after phone call, ordering their people to prepare. Outside, beyond Megg House and its grounds, members of the Home Guard would be awoken from their beds, as would members of the Army, ARP, Wrens, even the dear old Girl Guides. All would be rallied by the sharp rap on the door, the telephone call and, perhaps in time, the air raid siren itself.

"They could be heading for us, Sir; we've been told to stand by." A plotter bellowed the warning across the room. The stout men and women in uniform looked up for a moment before going back to their telephones. The duty supervisor was standing beside the Wren.

"How many settlements between us and them?" he asked.

"Three major towns, several minor ones, but some with airfields, Sir," she said. The other plotters stood back, waiting to hear if they would be needed.

Ten minutes passed. Sir stood over the map, his hands leaning against the edge, his body tipped forward. He stared at the map in front of him, each grid representing a place where someone was working, washing, cooking or sleeping, all united in the War effort. The Wren plotters gradually sat one by one against the back wall. Each one wore her headset, ready to react to a sighting. For a time only one stood by the map as she received reports of the formation of enemy planes. But as time passed another stood up, took up her plotting stick and began to do the same. A few minutes later she was followed by a third and then another and another. One raised her eyes to Sir's. "It looks like they're heading our way, Sir; they're definitely heading our way and there's a lot more than four now."

ENEMIES

2010

Arthur looked from one man to the other. What was going on? Mr Smith's breath had quickened. The two enemies, for that is what they appeared to be, continued staring at each other. The other figure spoke again.

"I've been waiting; bet you didn't expect that," he shouted. "I knew you'd come; a dog always returns to his vomit, isn't that right?"

He slowly, deliberately descended the stairs and began to walk towards them. Arthur stepped forward but felt Mr Smith's grip once again.

"It's all right, lad," he said. "It's time."

Arthur didn't know what he meant. Time for what? The other man was just a few steps away from them now and he was talking. "All these years, all these years," he hissed out the words. "I've been living up there, existing and waiting." He was in front of them now. "They thought I was going to die," he began pointing, "They told me I hadn't long to live, but I fought and I fought because I told myself I was going nowhere until I saw you again, until we had this out, you and me."

"How did you know we were here?" asked Mr Smith.

"I told you, I've lived for this moment," said the man. "I knew you'd come here. Well now it's happened, just you and me, as it always should have been, as it always had to be."

Mr Smith's voice was steady in reply. "And yet, now, after all this time, only I truly know who you are, Peach; only I know."

The other man swayed on his feet. "And only I know who *you* really are."

Mr Smith was calm. "And what's that?"

The stranger's eyes were bulging. "You're a spy, Brother, just a dirty, treacherous spy."

Mr Smith began to shuffle away from the man. He went over to a single wooden desk and bent down to sit on a nearby chair. "If we're going to do this now, then let's at least be civilised," he said.

The man was staring at Mr Smith leaning over him, but when he spoke his words were aimed at Arthur. "Did he tell you the truth, boy? Tell you about his past, did he? Let me guess, he failed to mention he's half-German. Our father, God rest him, was from Munich; did he mention it? Oh well, maybe he forgot. Or what about our mother, third generation to be born from Polish migrants? Funny, you don't look surprised." Arthur was about to reply when Mr Smith interrupted.

"I thought you must be dead, dear Brother, after all these years."

"Don't tell me, you were grieved," said Peach, his tone mocking. "I know enough about grief. What about Mamma and Papa? They were killed by the German bombing as well you know it. Smashed to smithereens

230

by their own countrymen, your friends, God rest them both."

Arthur was slowly beginning to understand. These two men were locked in a long-planned confrontation over events that stretched back well before he was even born, even before his own parents were born.

Peach continued to speak. "You told the Germans about the blackout flying, didn't you?" his voice was all of a sudden low and quiet with a tone so angry, so menacing that Arthur felt a shiver of real fear. "Well I hope you're happy," he continued, his eyes flaring.

"I didn't do it!" shouted Mr Smith.

Peach leant forward again towering over Mr Smith, "Carved our place in folklore then, didn't you, you and the wretched Luftwaffe." His voice was getting louder. His neck jutted out from his body under the strain of his own emotions, his secrets and his accusations.

The two men stared at each other, their eyes locked in a deep but bitter bond of those who have shared danger, escape, comradeship and above all betrayal.

Peach was the first to break the spell. "All those months, all those people looking for the German spies and their ringleader, and he was my own brother, my own brother! Not that good at it, though, were you," he sneared. "Almost got shot dead in the woods once, as I remember. Proper amateur."

Arthur looked towards Peach. "What do you mean?"

Mr Smith replied in a slow, deep voice. "He thinks I was the ringleader."

THE BOMBS

January 1941

Sir grabbed the phone on the duty supervisor's desk. "Put me through to the Intercept Room," he said sharply. Within seconds he was relaying orders. "All interceptors to switch to either German bomber frequencies or Orethorpe itself, looking for spy intercepts," he said. "Report immediately if you get anything."

He slammed the receiver down and walked over to the map. A Wren was standing nearby. "Warn those in the factories that it's not safe, do you understand?"

"Yes, Sir," she said in a crisp tone and jumped up the stairs and out of the room.

It was not long before news of the first bombers arrived. A young Wren stood by the map. She looked up. "Granvilles hit not five minutes ago, Sir," she said.

"Granvilles won't be the last!" he shouted.

"It isn't, Sir; there are already reports of aircraft at Gobley's!" one of the uniforms shouted back.

"Where's the RAF?" Sir was at the map now.

"They've sent up the five they've got left and others are being scrambled from Cox Hill," said another uniform.

"That will take forty minutes!" Sir shouted again.

One of the Wrens plotting on the map shouted out. "There are at least thirty German bombers now, Sir," she said. "Most are circling the town but some have already started on the factories as we know."

Just then another Wren raised her hand. "Two further hits on Granvilles reported, Sir," she said.

"They'll pick them off one by one," said Sir. "That's why they took the anti-aircraft guns out. That's why they took the ...."

His words were shattered by a great roar that split the air and detonated a great wall of noise. The walls of Number 10 shook and shuddered under the blast. Everyone dived under their desks, their chairs or the big map table. The shaking lasted several seconds before everything came to rest. Sir, Nancy, the Wrens and the other staff slowly began to recover from the shock. Dust and shards of paint were raining down from the ceiling. Out in the corridor was the sound of running footsteps hurrying towards the room.

For a moment Nancy really believed she was back home, lying on the floor of the privy on the night of the first bombing, the night she found the strange suitcase. As then, two arms scooped down and lifted her up: but they didn't belong to Father; they were a young officer's. He tried to stand her on her feet.

"Are you all right?" Sir was shouting at her; at least she thought he was, but he sounded far away somehow. He shouted again. She looked up. Several people were still on the floor, groping around for a table or chair to lever themselves up. Some of the older officers were already on their feet. Everyone wore a dazed expression. Nancy reached for Sir's hand to steady herself.

"I'm fine, I'm fine," she said. But just then her head began to feel fuzzy again and she began to sway.

"It looks like the house might have taken a direct hit, or maybe the grounds," said Sir. "Either way, we're quite safe down here in the basement."

A young Wren was standing by the map. She gently put her headphones back on and took up a plotting stick.

"Report," said Sir, approaching her.

"The RAF have engaged the enemy, Sir," she said. "Two fighter crews are engaged in a dogfight now."

"God speed to them, God speed," said Sir. It was the first time Nancy had heard him utter anything religious.

"Wait, Sir, wait: something else." By now the Wren had been joined by two others who had also managed to recover their wits from the shock of the blast.

"Well?" said Sir.

"A direct hit on Langleys, Sir. You were right: they're targeting the factories."

"How bad?"

"One direct hit and others circling, Sir. Those on the ground are trying to put out the fires now."

Sir turned towards the top row of desks. "Evacuate the factories." He turned back to the map.

"Any other civilian targets identified?"

"Not yet, Sir."

"What on earth happened upstairs? Have we been hit? Why don't we know by now?"

Just then the young voice of Tom shouted down from the top of the stairs. "A bomb has landed in the grounds in front of the house, Sir. The house and the huts are being evacuated: all except the Intercept Room and the

Direction Finding Hut, that is. They insist on staying put, Sir."

Sir smiled, but it was not a smile of pleasure, but a grim smile, one in recognition of an inescapable fact. "As I knew they would," he whispered to himself.

TRUTH

2010

Arthur looked across to Mr Smith. "You were a German spy during the War?"

Mr Smith flashed a look of anger at him. "How quick you are to believe the worst." He looked back at Peach. "Sorry to disappoint you, but as I told Peach here many, many years ago I was **not** a spy, nowhere close. I was a military intelligence operative, MI5 as it is still called, and I was ordered to infiltrate the real German spy ring. Not that he would listen."

"You were seen with that teacher; she was a spy, wasn't she?" shouted Peach. "You were out in the woods that night. You were in contact with them: more than that, you were the one we were really looking for, the ringleader, the most dangerous spy of all. Ha, what a joke. My own brother. I knew it then and I know it now."

"You know nothing! I told you, I was on your side. I was working for MI5; so was Miss Temple. You also knew her, very well as I recall. We were trying to *infiltrate* the spy ring, not *join* it."

"And now, just as then, you offer no proof, Brother, no proof at all."

Mr Smith's face grew red. "I am your brother, you shouldn't have needed proof!" He was shouting. "I told you the truth that time on the station platform. I told you about me, about Miss Temple, but you wouldn't listen, that's why I ran away. I still had a job to do. We weren't traitors, we were never traitors, but you didn't believe it, wouldn't believe it."

"You were almost caught, that's why you said it."

"Our radio messages down to HQ in London were being intercepted by you lot. And just as we were getting close to identifying the spies, the Germans started to get suspicious. MI5 wanted to pull us out, saying we couldn't take the risk, but we had a job to do."

"And how did you know we were intercepting you?"

"We had our own man here in Megg House as well, or didn't they tell you? Another Polish volunteer in fact; he knew we had to know what you were doing if we were to stay one step ahead."

"He was feeding you information."

"Well MI5 didn't trust you to get the job done in time. They had to have people on the ground, all the more so because of what was going on up at Langleys."

Peach staggered back and collapsed into a chair. He leant forward, putting his head in his hands. He mumbled something which Arthur didn't hear and so he asked him to say it again.

"You'll never understand what I went through trying to protect you," he repeated. "The silence, the lies I was prepared to tell after I saw you that night when the railway line was bombed. The sleepless nights, knowing I was a traitor, putting family above everything else. I was working around the clock to read every intercept, trying to find you, to get to you before they did, to warn you. I even drove a car through the German spies' roadblock knowing I'd probably be killed. That's why I confronted you that last time on the railway platform. That's why I told you that you had to go, to get away or I wouldn't have any choice but to let them arrest you. So don't talk to me of loyalty, Brother, of betrayal, because I betrayed everything for you and it has haunted me ever since, ever since." He lowered his head into his hands once more.

Mr Smith slumped back in his chair and slowly replied. "As you have haunted me, Brother, as you have haunted me."

ANOTHER MESSAGE

January 1941

Much later, some of those inside Number 10 that terrible night would try to piece together the order of events. They would go over and over the hours and minutes, piece by piece, and write a great list of when a telephone call was received, a piece of information relayed, another mark placed upon the map in the centre of the room. When did the news come in that the first of the RAF planes had been shot down? When did they know that one had landed in the middle of the Summers Field estate? What of the German bombers? Who was it that telephoned in the sighting of the bombs raining down upon Langleys? Did they learn about that first, or was it after someone had taken the call about the fires and fires upon fires raging at Granvilles and amongst the many terraced houses on the other side of the railway line, not half a mile away? Later, didn't a schoolboy tell some journalists that he'd stood and watched the dogfight between the Germans and the RAF in the clear night sky? A single Spitfire had suddenly burst into the fray. The schoolboy had watched the planes dive and curve before one of them began to cough and spit, smoke and flames trailing from the rear as it whined and dived to the ground, finally hitting the railway bank with a terrifying force.

After the shock of the blast everyone inside Number 10 was soon back on their feet. Positions had been retaken, telephones rang out again. Several Wrens stood over the map in front of them marking the positions of enemy aircraft. Bombs were being dropped over factories and warehouses, houses and shops.

"They're making mincemeat of the place!" shouted Sir. "We should have prevented this; we should have stopped it."

"Wait, Sir, there's something else coming through!" shouted a Wren.

Everyone looked across towards her. She looked up again. "The RAF are here, Sir; they've come now."

"Too late, too late, I have to speak to London!" Sir shouted. He rushed for the stairs. "Nancy," he shouted back, "ring me upstairs with progress, understand?" With that he sprinted away.

Minutes later one of the older men in uniform began to shout Nancy's name. He was standing on the upper level, a telephone receiver in one hand. "The Intercept Room needs you," he shouted down to her.

She quickly made her way upstairs. Entering the Intercept Room, she saw tables and chairs on one side, papers strewn across the carpet and the curtains billowing in the winter wind. The force of the earlier blast had smashed the windows and shaken the earth beneath the entire building. Only a few tables had been put back on their feet. Behind them sat interceptors.

"We're desperately short of people, so get intercepting," said the supervisor.

One of the men in the room helped her to stand a table back up. He lifted the receiver box off the floor and retrieved a chair. The box was still operational. Nancy went through the usual routine; headphones on, pen and paper at the ready, the dial turned to the right frequency. The freezing night air wrapped itself around her small body. It brought with it the deep, intense smell of fires. The town was taking a hammering. Nancy's heart lurched as she looked out of the broken window, into the darkness. The air had jolted her out of the world of Megg House and back across the town, where Mother, Father, Mary, Audrey, Joyce and Kep and all the others were. What was happening to them? Had they made it to the shelters in time? Were they alive?

The supervisor appeared behind her shoulder as Nancy bent over the desk. She squeezed her eyes tightly together to shut off the real world and strained to enter the unreal, electronic one of the intercept set. Immediately the sight of the injured woman's face danced before her imagination. She bent forward further. The hiss of the radio provided little distraction. There was no message being relayed, at least not at first. Nancy's thoughts switched back to her parents and sisters. She longed to spring up from the desk, rush out of Megg House and down towards the town. But something held her there, duty perhaps, or something else.

She was not thinking of the spies or their murderous messages when the bleeps and blips began to emerge from the heavy hiss in her headphones. But the sound of it jolted her back to the receiver set. Something was coming through. It was slow and then fast. What's more, it wasn't encrypted. There was a pause and then it would start again. She raised her hand and a supervisor approached. Any moment now the presence on the airwaves would be gone, she knew that. But it lingered. She glanced down at the dial; it was the same frequency as before. Something else was familiar: the same message was being repeated over and over. It went on and on, over and over. Whoever was sending the message was sending it again and again, staying on air minute after minute. It made no sense. Did they assume the vans wouldn't be operational during an air raid? Maybe the operator believed that the strike on Megg House had wiped out any risk of detection.

"I'll alert direction finding," the supervisor shouted, running to the telephone on her desk.

Still the message came, again and again until, finally, the hiss grew louder and the bleeps, the dits and the dots grew fainter, more spread out. Then, they stopped altogether. Nancy swivelled around to face the supervisor. She stood, still holding the telephone. One nod of the head told her that they had a lock on the signal. Nancy grabbed the wad of paper containing the intercepted message and ran out of the room. She sprinted across the hall and heaved the front door open.

Red smoke from a hundred fires streaked across the night sky. She closed the front door behind her and turned towards the drive. A car had pulled up; the engine was still running. She walked over to the driver's seat. Inside, slumped over, was Peach. His shoulders shook and he began to punch the steering wheel. Nancy saw tears streaking down his cheeks. She wondered what he was doing but she couldn't stop to confront him for she had to get to the Direction Finding Hut on the far side of the lawn. When she reached them the crew was already in the van. "Take me with you, take me with you," she pleaded. They didn't have time to argue as she jumped into the back. Seconds later they were speeding away.

STALEMATE

2010

The room was in silence. Standing between the men, Arthur looked from one to another. Neither moved. Arthur began to walk around the room. Great dusty boards lay askew on the walls. He accidentally kicked a wooden stick and it clattered underfoot. He pulled up a filthy chair and sat down and glanced at some dust covered papers. He was startled by Peach's voice.

"Well if you weren't the one tipping them off, who was?"

"Wasn't it your job to find out, Brother?" Mr Smith replied. "Trouble is, MI5 didn't think you were up to it. Turns out they were right."

"Yes, perhaps they were."

"So there were German spies in Orethorpe during the War?" asked Arthur to neither one of them, but both of them at the same time.

Mr Smith glanced across towards his brother. "Yes, but I wasn't one of them, whatever he tells you."

Arthur looked between the two men again. Mr Smith just stared ahead, but when he looked over towards the man called Peach, Arthur could see huge tears had begun to break out from his tired eyes and were streaking down his sunken cheeks. Eventually he wiped them away and turned to the boy.

"It wasn't just about the factories," he said to Arthur. "The spies wanted to destroy the factories and also get at what was in them."

"War machinery and stuff?" asked Arthur.

"Well, that and, well, other reasons," replied Peach. He paused a moment before he shrugged his shoulders and went on. "*This* has never been declassified, but I will tell you anyway. Langleys wasn't just making stuff for the War effort, it was being used to hold captured German agents and high-ranking German prisoners of War. They built a special hangar for them, made out it was part of the factory even though no-one actually working there was allowed to go near it. About thirty Germans were there, all under tight security. Each time some of them were moved there would be a secret mission to get them out unnoticed, especially by the German agents on the ground working in the town. That's the real reason the spies were here, as well as telling the Germans what we were making here. This town truly was the front line of the War in that way: making vital equipment to win it and also acting as a secret prison for those who had fallen into our hands."

"You got them out of there safe though, not one of them was freed," said Mr Smith, his voice weak.

Peach turned back to face his brother. "Yes we did, but when they had all finally gone they didn't hesitate to blitz us all to the ground, did they? No risk of killing any of their own then."

"As you say," said Mr Smith, "Once the last had gone, there was nothing to stop them from unleashing the bombers, which I am sure they relished. It was their own form of punishment, theirs and theirs alone."

Exhausted, the two men fell silent and simply stared emptily into the distance. Eventually, Mr Smith pulled himself up and reached out for Arthur's hand. He wearily climbed the steps and left Peach alone in the room, deep in his own thoughts.

Arthur and Mr Smith returned the way they had come and managed to return to the reunion room unnoticed before they quickly left the house. Walking home, Arthur was still confused but could see that Mr Smith was in no mood to talk, but he did say one thing, "I promise you a full explanation but not today, not today."

NANCY'S DISCOVERY

January 1941

Nancy peered through the back window of the van as it sped along. The town's streets were filthy with dust and debris. Many buildings stood untouched but many more had been punctured, punched or squashed back into the earth, their glass and metal insides squeezed out into the pavements and roads. Smoke and flames were everywhere.

Deeply shocked people were wondering everywhere, forcing the van to brake sharply several times. People in uniform were ordering and rounding up those in nightclothes. The newly-homeless couples clung to each other, held hands and squeezed their children to their bodies. Ambulances moved between the crowds and everyone was moved along by the volunteers holding out blankets and kind hands.

The van made its way through the chaos and din. It continued to the end of the road before turning a sharp left, jolting Nancy to the side. Moments later the wheels slowed and then suddenly stopped. The front doors were quickly opened and slammed shut. Running footsteps passed the back window. She raised herself up on her arm and lurched herself towards the back door of the van. She wrenched it open and jumped out.

At first she couldn't think where the men had gone. A small row of terraced houses stood in front of her. It was the swinging gate that led her to one of the neat houses along the row.

The house was dark and silent, but approaching the front door she noticed that it was on the latch. She pushed it open. What she assumed to be the living room was also unlit but she could see a small light coming from the kitchen. Nancy walked towards it. Upstairs she could hear the men running from room to room, their boots stomping along the floorboards, trampling down the rugs and mats.

Inside the kitchen there was a group of cracked mugs on a worktop. She walked over to the stove and reached out her hand. It was still warm. Someone had been here very recently. The stomping upstairs had been replaced by thunder on the staircase. Nancy called out to the men, telling them where she was.

"You shouldn't be here love, this is dangerous," one shouted at her, upon entering the kitchen.

"Look," she said, ignoring the rebuke, "someone's been here recently, the stove is still warm."

"Well they're not here now."

"What now, boss?" The second man appeared in the doorway.

"We have to get back, damn it," said the first man.

They both turned to walk back towards the open front door. Nancy glanced over the kitchen once more. No, there were no more clues. She turned to leave but as she did so a tiny light flashed briefly before her eyes. It came through the back window of the kitchen.

"Wait!" she exclaimed. "I can see something!"

She leant forward, peering into the blackness outside. The light had gone. It did not return. "There's something out there," she shouted.

"There's a lot out there at the moment love, and none of it pretty," said the first man.

But Nancy did not bother to listen. She yanked open the back door of the kitchen and stepped out into the yard. Even with the glow of the fires overhead she could barely make out the outline of the yard. "Get a torch, someone," she shouted behind her shoulder.

The second man quickly appeared with a torch in one hand. He flashed it along the back wall of the yard, tracing the greasy brickwork until, halfway up the yard, it came to the ancient-looking wooden door of a shed or outhouse. "It's just the outside toilet," he said.

Nancy stepped forward. The man with the torch followed. She hesitated, her heart was thumping, her body trembling. The rumble of a bomber plane overhead made her body jolt, but instead of jangling her nerves even more, it seemed to steady them. She returned her gaze towards the door of the outhouse and reached for the latch. It was smooth and sprung back easily. The door did not even creak. Behind her one of the men flashed his light into the black abyss. It was not a toilet but a small, wooden shed. The torch illuminated the enclosed space and it did not take them long to rest upon the sole occupant of the room. Miss Halsall had retreated to the back wall. Tears streamed down her cheeks and, in the woman's trembling hands Nancy saw a simple, small gun.

"Get away, get away!" shouted Miss Halsall. In that moment it would have been impossible for anyone to say who was the most shocked, the most afraid; the woman with the gun or the girl and the two men facing her.

"Come off it, you're not going to shoot her, a girl," shouted one of the men behind her.

Miss Halsall looked over at Nancy. "I would, I would if she's a traitor," she shouted.

Nancy heard one of the men inch his way past her but she continued to stare at Miss Halsall. "I'm no traitor, you're the traitor," she said eventually. But no-one heard her words, for Miss Halsall had begun to shout again at the man's advance.

"Get back, get back!" she screamed.

But still the man closed in on her. "Got that thing loaded, have we?" he asked, his tone almost mocking.

"I told you to get back!"

"And I'm telling you to put that thing down."

"I found them, I found them," screamed Miss Halsall.

"Found who, then?" asked the man.

"The spies! What do you think?"

"And here's me thinking you're one of them," said the man, inching ever closer.

The man still standing behind Nancy began to move his feet. As he did so he seemed to catch his foot on something. He swayed forward, pushing against Nancy, before he swayed backwards on his heels. He fell towards the wall close to the door. He must have hit a light switch for, as he fell to the ground, the room suddenly became flooded with the intense yellow of a naked light bulb hanging from the ceiling. The shock was enough to distract Miss Halsall, causing her to raise her hand to shield her eyes. As she did so the other man leapt forward and seized her arm holding the gun with his large hands. He forced her elbow back, causing her to yelp in pain. The gun clattered to the floor. He held her body now and was forcing her to the ground. Nancy blinked as she watched Miss Halsall submit to his superior strength. The other man leapt forward to help and together they secured her arms tightly behind her back.

"It's not me, it's not me!" she was shouting.

"Tell them that up at Megg House," shouted one of the men. "And explain that thing as well."

Nancy didn't know what he meant. But, just then, she saw it. The stained, brown leather suitcase had been balanced on an upturned bucket. A low stool, the kind used for milking cows, was beside it. Inside the case was the unmistakable paraphernalia of a transmitter set.

They dragged her across the floor and out towards the yard. Passing Nancy, Miss Halsall began to shout again. "Tell Sir I found them, tell Sir, tell Sir," she shouted towards Nancy.

Moments later she was being taken up the yard, towards the house and van.

"I'm sure they will be very pleased to see you," said one of the men to Miss Halsall.

"None more so than Sir," thought Nancy to herself as the van sped off to Megg House.

Suddenly, left alone and with all the excitement over, Nancy's thoughts turned to her family. How were they faring in all this horror? Without a second thought, she started to run as fast as she could, ignoring all the devastation around her. On turning the final corner she shed tears of joy to see their row of houses undamaged. She felt an inward lurch of relief to see the family as well as the neighbours standing in the street. They were alive, they were alive. She ran up to them and they hugged each other, unashamed of the tears.

KEP

1941

Several hours earlier Sergeant Keiren Harris, always known to his friends and family as Kep, had climbed into his Stirling four-engine bomber plane. He was the pilot. Alongside him served the navigator, bomb aimer, flight engineer, wireless operator, mid-upper gunner and rear gunner. The Stirling did not travel light, but it was not supposed to. It was built to bomb. Tonight they were not loaded down with any armaments; this was purely a practice: blackout, low flying exercise. But it was notoriously hazardous and something every pilot dreaded. Kep was no exception.

He checked his instruments and waited for the all-clear. Within a few minutes the Stirling was speeding down the runway and then roaring through the air. From a thousand feet Orethorpe was scarcely visible but from three hundred feet it was possible to make out the shapes of the roofs below.

The first circle of the town went well. He had lowered the nose of the plane down as far as he dared allow and almost hovered for a moment before he sped over the town. He was a surfer riding a low wave, the foam and spray of the sea splashing onto his board.

A command came through on his headset. They were to go again. Kep rounded the plane in the sky and dived for a second time, the other planes behind him following his lead. As he came in low again, the dials in front of him disappeared in a sudden burst of glare. For several seconds the light washed out every trace of the scene in front of him. Moments later it was gone, only to return. He was flying into the searchlights of the anti-aircraft stations.

He pulled up too quickly, making the engine whine and moan. The men onboard cried out. The light had ceased to follow him, but after he had turned the plane around he saw it catch one of the other planes behind him, like a torch shining on a moth.

He headed back to base. He landed the plane with a rough thud and was out of the seat almost before the engine had stopped. He ripped off his headset and goggles and ran up to his Commanding Officer, the other crew members scrambling after him.

"What on earth happened up there?" he shouted. "Haven't you warned them?"

The man lowered his binoculars. "We told them it was us; they were warned earlier today. It must be some catastrophe in communications. But keep your hair on, it's just another opportunity to practice your ducking and avoidance skills."

Two more Stirlings had followed him onto the tarmac. The crews withdrew from them and began to run. "They're shooting us down. Someone tell them to lay off." They gabbled out the words in high-pitched voices.

"They're what? What the devil do you mean?"

"The anti-aircraft guns. Someone down there thinks we're German. Almost didn't make it out at all."

They made their way into the operations hut. Inside the Commanding Officer grabbed hold of a telephone receiver and demanded answers. Kep and the others stood around for several minutes. Then the terrible news came in. One of the Stirlings had gone down. Several minutes later another message was relayed. Another had taken a direct hit; the pilot, the rest of the crew and the plane itself were almost certainly lost.

Kep staggered back on his feet. How could this have happened, he thought to himself? How could the town's own anti-aircraft guns have been turned on them?

The Commanding Officer continued to slam down and pick up the telephone receiver, each time demanding answers, but updates were slow to come through. Eventually he lowered the receiver from his mouth, his features frozen. "The anti-aircraft stations have been sabotaged," he said.

Everyone stopped to look around. "Sabotaged, by what?" shouted one of the pilots in the room.

"Don't you mean by whom? By them, of course, the Germans. We were warned there might be spies about and this confirms it again."

A long time passed before the assembled group received more news. There were reports of German bombers over the skies of Orethorpe. Without the cover of the anti-aircraft guns the town was almost defenseless.

Immediately Kep's mind turned to the single Spitfire on the base. He turned to his Commanding Officer.

"Let me go up in the Spit, Sir; I can try to hold them off until the others get here."

"Are you insane, man? They'll have you down in less than a minute."

Kep turned to another man on the telephone. "How many did you say there were?"

"Five so far," he replied.

Kep turned back to his Commanding Officer. "I can try to distract them."

"Absolutely out of the question: we wait for reinforcements, is that clear?"

Kep saluted and turned to leave the hut. He walked across the grass and towards the runway. The Spitfire was on the other side, close to an old hangar. An engineer was working on it and looked up when he approached.

"I'm taking her out to see what's going on," said Kep. "Hand me the helmet, will you."

"It's in the cockpit," replied the engineer. He leant upright and stared at Kep.

"It's okay to fly, I'm only tinkering, but what are you doing with her? You're a bomber boy, aren't you?"

"Not right now," said Kep.

He climbed into the plane and quickly snapped on his helmet. Knowing he could be discovered any moment, he began to rush the pre-take-off checks. Glancing across the runway he could see it remained clear. But for how long?

The engine leapt into life, so much nimbler than the bombers. Within a few minutes it was racing down the runway, away from the huts. He pulled on the throttle and the plane swept into the air. He was airborne for just ten minutes when he first saw them, far more planes than had been originally reported were sliding gracefully along like migrating birds in the air. He knew he had been spotted quickly, for one broke off and veered right before coming behind him. He ducked fast as if he had taken a direct hit. The bomber tried to follow but was slowed down by its bulk. Kep came up sharply once again, this time behind the formation. They were almost over Orethorpe.

Suddenly one of the bombers broke formation again. He was followed by a second. They swirled around in an arc on each side of the Spitfire before coming up behind. Kep pulled up the plane and glanced downwards. Plumes of fire and black smoke were already rising from the ground below. The German bombers had begun their barrage of the town.

The first bullets splattered into his plane from the right. Further planes were now on his tail. He swirled up and around again to face them. It was then that he got another shock for some these weren't bombers. Some were German Messerschmitts Bf 109's, the equivalent of the Spitfire. Three of them were facing him. Moments later several further lines of bullets raced towards his plane. He managed to duck before arcing to the left, but they were at his tail again in just a few moments. He rounded again to come to their back, but they followed him. Pulling up, he realised he was facing another direct confrontation. It was this or making a sharp dive and trying to wriggle free. He clenched his hands around the instruments and held back his head. The next moment he was racing into the deadly metal storm ahead.

THREE WEEKS AFTER THE RETURN TO MEGG HOUSE

January 2010

The bus ride out of town was much the same as it was before. This time Arthur and Mr Smith had known which way to turn and where to walk to reach the cemetery. But, unlike before, they didn't stop at the gate; they passed through it and advanced down the drive until they came to a small chapel. The chapel sat in the middle of a wide expanse of land, all covered in row upon row of headstones. Only when they reached it did Arthur turn to Mr Smith to speak.

"Do you know what you're looking for?" he asked.

To his surprise the old man smiled widely. "A little peace of mind, perhaps, and forgiveness," he said.

"The dead can't forgive someone," said Arthur.

Mr Smith reached over and tousled his hair. "No, but we can ask anyway."

The door to the chapel opened and a young vicar emerged. "There aren't any services or anything booked in today," he called over to them.

"No, we know; we're just here to pay our respects," shouted Mr Smith. The vicar nodded. "Is the chapel open for a bit?"

"For the next half-hour, yes, but then I've got to lock up and go."

Mr Smith smiled and waved his hand in thanks. "Best get out of the cold, eh?" he said to Arthur.

The chapel was dark and the air smelt stale, reminding Arthur of his first visit to Mr Smith's house. His friend looked serious again and the frailty of old age had returned to him. A great bond had been forged between them since their visit to Megg House.

They sat, side by side, in front of the small altar of the chapel. Arthur wasn't afraid of silence and was content to sit alone with his thoughts, but eventually Mr Smith began to tell him the whole mystery.

"We were brothers, both born in Manchester. Our father was German you see. He came over to Britain with his mother before the first Great War, but his brother fought on the German side.

"Our own mother was from a Polish immigrant family and they weren't too pleased when she got a German surname."

Arthur's mind turned over. "But Smith isn't German; it's English," he said before suddenly remembering his visit to the library.

Mr Smith chuckled. "No, my lad, my real name is Schmitt, the German surname for Smith. So is my brother's. He changed it to Smith during the War, and soon acquired the nickname Peach. I changed mine later. Well it's a very common name, isn't it? Easy to get lost in a crowd with that one."

Arthur gazed up at the chapel's only stained glass window. Its colours would be brilliant when the full bloom of the summer sunshine came streaming in. But today the greens had been turned to a muddy brown and the reds to the dark, sickly colour of blood. The pieces, put in place so many years ago, were prepared and ready to show their true worth, but without the sun they could only wait.

He turned back to Mr Smith. "Why didn't you keep in contact with him? Is it because he thought you were a German spy?"

"He was a brilliant student, much like me," replied the old man. "I went to Oxford to read History and German and he went to Cambridge to read Maths. That's how he came to be at Megg House, on account of his mathematical ability: not that he was happy with that, I gather. He wanted to be at Bletchley Park, where the really advanced work was being done, and, well, let's not get into that.

"When the War broke out I was called into MI5, and he, well, I didn't know then what he was doing and we drifted apart. He told our parents that it was hush-hush work and we believed him; well, I did, as I was the same." He turned to Arthur. "So how was it that we came to be in the same town? I've asked that myself many times and can only think it was sheer coincidence."

"Here, when?"

"During the War," replied Mr Smith. "He was at Megg House trying to catch German spies and then, one day, while on the brink of actually catching one, who does he see running out of the fog against a hail of bullets? Me, his own brother, for goodness' sake." He began shuffling his feet and twisting his hands.

"So you were a spy, then?" asked Arthur.

"So he believed. It was his job to catch them, but how could he turn in his own brother? He tracked me down and told me that I had to leave the German service and get out of Orethorpe, or he would arrest me and I would be shot for sure. I kept asking him how he could accuse his own brother and that he had to trust me. It was a terrible situation for both of us."

"What happened?"

"We had a furious row at a deserted railway station outside Orethorpe and then, not long later, they came."

"Who came?"

"The German bombers."

Mr Smith leant forward and placed his head in his hands. It was several minutes before he spoke again.

"They annihilated us. All I could do was listen, hour after hour, to the terrible bombs going off and the screams and the cries, all the while knowing it was my fault; it was my terrible fault. We should have stopped them."

Arthur didn't understand. Why was it his fault? He was on the right side, the side of good. It wasn't his fault there were German spies.

"I knew it was my fault," continued Mr Smith, "We were given everything, money, men and women, cover: we should have tracked them. We could have prevented it. And looking into Peach's eyes the other week I saw he felt the same guilt, the same shame. He hadn't been able to stop it either."

Arthur saw Mr Smith's tears splash onto the stone slabs of the chapel. It was many moments before he straightened himself up. He took out a handkerchief and wiped his eyes.

"Our parents died during the War, they were bombed in Manchester, and there was no other family left. So I never saw him after the attack on Orethorpe: well, not until the other week, but you know all about that."

"Hello, Brother."

The voice broke through the still silence of the chapel. They hadn't heard the door open but turned and were very surprised to see another figure walking down the aisle towards them. It was Peach. Mr Smith rose to his feet and spun around.

"So you came?" he said.

"I almost didn't," replied Peach.

Mr Smith pulled open his bag. He reached down and held up what looked like a file. He walked towards his brother. "Here," he said, thrusting it at Peach, "my War record, recently declassified, telling the truth for once and for all."

Peach did not take the file offered to him, but Mr Smith continued to hold it out towards him in an act of defiance.

"It tells you who the spies really were, if you want to know," he said. "You might recognise one or two of the names, especially one in particular. A Miss Halsall she was called, at least to you."

Arthur watched Peach stagger back. His lips began to tremble as he reached out for a chair to steady himself.

"I'm not surprised you were never told," said Mr Smith. "It was too humiliating for the 'top brass' to admit that, of course. Besides, it would have caused a riot, what with all the deaths, injuries, bloodshed and grief from the bombings. How could they explain that to the homeless and the bereaved; that one of their own was responsible? The town, or what was left of it, would have turned into a mob."

Still Peach said nothing. But then, slowly, he began to shuffle close to Mr Smith who did not move but stood staring at his brother. For a moment Arthur wondered if Peach was about to strike the other man. He stepped forward but at that moment Peach did something that defied his advanced age. He raised his arms and grabbed his brother, pulling him close to him. Arthur heard sobs come from one man and then the other. There they stood in each others arms. After several minutes they pulled away, each reaching into their pockets for something with which to soak away the tears.

"I forgive you, Brother, as I forgive myself," said Peach, his voice trembling.

Mr Smith simply held out the file to him again. Peach opened the file with shaking hands. Arthur went and stood next to them. Peering down he saw that there was a photograph of a very young woman dressed in some kind of uniform. A second photograph showed a man dressed in a shirt and tie and a smart pullover. As well as the photographs there were papers, many papers. All were stamped TOP SECRET or CLASSIFIED. Peach slumped back in the chair he had used for support and began to read. After a few minutes he looked up.

"I was with you all the time, Brother: do you believe me now?" whispered Mr Smith.

"Yes," Peach whispered back. He gulped hard. "Miss Halsall?" he asked. "We were told she had suddenly been transferred to other top secret work and we never heard from her again."

Mr Smith replied: "They were all under her command. She was the ringleader, she was the most dangerous spy of all. You knew her, a lot of you did, up at Megg House. She was arrested, but those who knew were sworn to secrecy. She was interrogated but she played for time and made sure that others had enough of a chance to escape before she said anything. They shot her, of course. Well, she couldn't be allowed to live after that. All hushed up it was. The 'top brass' couldn't risk that getting out."

Peach began to sob again. "And the others?" he asked.

"It's all in there as you can see, not that you'd recognise any of their names I expect. Someone called Jack Jones and others. Some melted away back into the chaos of that terrible night of the bombing. Some were killed."

"We were both on the right side in the end," said Peach.

"Yes we were," said Mr Smith, "Yes we were."

They embraced again.

Afterwards

2010

Mr Smith never returned to the cemetery, or to Megg House. Six months later he moved into a newly built care home on the edge of the town. Once, when visiting early one Saturday morning, Arthur had found him in the corner of the large lounge talking with someone. Assuming it to be another resident Arthur had sprinted up to the semi-circle of chairs. He was surprised to see the face of Mr Smith's brother smiling up at him. It was one of the last times he saw them together and one of the last times he saw Mr Smith for the old man died a few weeks later. The warden of the home drew Arthur into her office one visit and told him the news. Mr Smith had passed away peacefully in the night. There hadn't been any suffering. Mum and Dad attended the funeral with him and, apart from a couple of other folk, it was a poor affair for both attendance and remembrances. "All his secrets are held by the dead, well, most of them," thought Arthur. He had craned his neck around the small church to see if Mr Smith's brother had come, but he wasn't there. But then, as they were leaving, Arthur spotted his stooped figure in the corner of the back row. He didn't look up as the boy and his parents passed by.

Mr Smith had indeed hidden his secrets from the town he had called home for so long. And yet, even in death he revealed one last thing to his special friend. A week after the funeral Arthur returned home to find a large, brown envelope on the stairs. "Delivered by the care home, addressed to you," said Mother. Arthur took it upstairs to his room and closed the door. The envelope was bulky and heavy. He slit open the top with a pen. Immediately wafer-like flakes of old newspaper cuttings began to spill out. Most were newspaper reports of the War. They told of Allied victories and then defeats. The smeared, yellowing paper and blurred typeface of the Orethorpe Gazette was amongst the copies. It told the full horrors of that dreadful night of annihilation. Photographs of the night showed towers of flames and smoke. More, taken in the days after, captured the survivors, the grieving, the homeless and the shell-shocked standing beside caved-in homes or giant craters in the streets, people bedded down in state shelters and queuing to bury their dead.

Arthur pulled at the contents of the envelope again. More cuttings spilled out onto the carpet. There, amongst them, was something thicker, newer. He reached out to read it. It wasn't from the time of the War, it was from much later. It was also from the local newspaper. Arthur read it silently.

ORETHORPE GAZETTE, JUNE 7TH, 1992
OBITUARIES SECTION

Nancy Stewart, nee Brown, 1929-1992

The Orethorpe Gazette is sad to announce the death of one of its most distinguished but sadly uncelebrated daughters.

Nancy Stewart, born Nancy Brown in 1929, was the youngest of three daughters of a factory worker and housewife.

During the Second World War she proved herself to be an accomplished Girl Guide and aided Orethorpe with the many skills of that organisation. But it was her talent at Morse code and shortwave radio that, it is believed, brought her to the attention of the authorities.

Many of the records of that time remain classified, but enough is known to say that she became an interceptor tracing enemy spy communications over the radio waves. Much of this was carried out at Megg House, which was covered in a cloud of secrecy at the time. Many townsfolk had staff from the house billeted at their homes but were never allowed a glimpse into this secretive world.

Like her fellow workers, Nancy Brown signed the Official Secrets Act and set about aiding the house in detecting the spies and trying to ascertain if they were operating within Orethorpe itself. Not enough is known about their success in doing so but the devastating bombing of Orethorpe in January 1941 has been recorded in history as a failure of Megg House to prevent such destruction and loss of life. It was closed immediately after, fenced off and quietly ignored for many years until redeveloped as an old people's home. Since then some of those who worked there at the time have successfully corrected the record with new insights into the work of intercepting radio waves. They have talked of the house's role in providing vital intercepts to Bletchley Park which is now known to have been a hive of brilliant and innovative code breaking. Some even say that the work carried out at Bletchley Park helped shorten the War and save millions of lives.

In a rare interview about her work at Megg House recorded in 1986, Nancy Stewart, as she was then known, spoke about the events of that dreadful January night in 1941. She said:

"I was at Megg House when the reports came in about the German bombers advancing on the town. It was a terrible moment after so many months of trying to find the spies and disrupt their work. That was our real job you see. That very night I took a message about something that finally helped us track down one of the spies. That very night we tracked the signal. But, well, let's just say there was a terrible shock to be had that night, for all of us at the house."

More light was shed on this secret episode by Mrs Joyce Cavendish, who grew up in the house next door to the Browns. The two girls enjoyed a close friendship. One day, while giving a talk to a group of schoolgirls, Mrs Cavendish revealed that, incredibly, her own home had indeed been home to a German spy, quite unknown to her family at the time. Our account of what she said is taken from an article published in this newspaper, covering the event.

"To us he was a considerate boarder who worked at one of the factories and who gave his spare time to work as a civilian dispatch rider, taking messages around the town when it was under attack," she said.

"On the night of that terrible bombing me and my family were in the air raid shelter for hours before we saw these policemen coming towards us. They got Mother out of the shelter even though we were in the middle of the most terrible attack. It was truly terrifying.

They took Mother back to our house and there was Mr Jones stood there. She was asked to identify him, which she did, and then she was told that he was a German spy who had admitted to hiding his equipment in, of all places, next door's outside loo! She couldn't believe it."

Mrs Cavendish's eldest brother, Kep, short for Kieren, was killed in a dogfight with the German planes that same night and posthumously given a VC for his selfless bravery. Mrs Cavendish herself passed away last year.

Miss Brown's talents meant that, although still young, but with her parents' permission, she continued working for the Government during the War, although not in Orethorpe itself. Many years later she revealed that she had worked in London, and later abroad, but no more is known at this stage and it is this newpaper's opinion that the secrets of her later War work should not have been carried to her grave.

After the War, Miss Brown was recruited as a full-time agent and distinguished herself during the Cold War, although even less is known about this period of her career, for obvious reasons. After returning to Britain she continued to climb through the ranks of the service until, in 1980, she received the Distinguished Service Order award from the Queen.

She married and had two daughters. She never returned to Orethorpe to live, only to visit. She was sometimes seen standing on the front lawns of Megg House, looking towards the building, perhaps remembering the extraordinary events that occurred within its walls, many of which have sadly disappeared into history.

Arthur put the cutting down and stood up. He walked over to the window and scanned the landscape beyond the row of houses. He knew that trauma had turned to memory and then into history. One day, he thought, I'll try to bring it back, as much of it as I can, I'll find anyone still alive before it's too late, search through the records, unearth their secret past and finally write their story. People have to know, they have to appreciate their work and they must always remember the sacrifice of the dead.

He turned back around and began to scoop up the cuttings as if they were as precious as bank notes. He briefly hugged the pile before placing it into the top drawer of his bedside cabinet and gently pushed it shut.

THE END

Author's Notes

Upon the outbreak of the Second World War the British authorities knew that it would be vital to detect and listen into enemy radio transmissions so the Radio Security Service (RSS) was created. Its job was to "intercept, locate and close down" illicit wireless stations operated by "enemy agents in Great Britain". Enemy agents meant, for the most part, German and Italian spies.

The RSS recruited amateur radio enthusiasts as Voluntary Interceptors (VIs). In 'The Most Dangerous Spy', Nancy Brown's father is recruited as one such interceptor. Reports differ as to how many VIs were ultimately recruited, but all sources agree that the number was more than a thousand and up to one-and-a-half thousand. They were mostly men, working at home on their own equipment. Some, such as Bob King who has since spoken of his experiences, were just youngsters no more than sixteen. Some VIs were even issued with special identity cards allowing them to enter premises where they suspected unauthorised signals were being transmitted.

However, it soon became clear that there were no enemy agents transmitting from the UK. But the work of the RSS and indeed the VIs was far from over. Instead, they were given the job of monitoring signals abroad, particularly messages from the German military intelligence organisation, the Abwehr.

Logs were sent to Arkley View, a house in the London Borough of Barnet. There they were sorted and eventually sent to Bletchley Park (Station X) for decryption, either by dispatch rider or, later, by teleprinter. In 'The Most Dangerous Spy' the character of Peach is seen on a motorbike taking intercepts down to Bletchley Park. Later in the book he drives down, taking Nancy Brown with him.

By 1941 Arkley View was receiving thousands of sheets from VIs each day and the Government decided to set up a 24-hour listening station. This was created at Hanslope Park in Buckinghamshire. There, full-time listeners, aided by the work of the VIs, listened into the German intelligence signals. The RSS became, in effect, a civilian outpost of the military Y Service – the service for intercepting and decoding enemy signals. Eventually the RSS was put under the authority of the Secret Intelligence Service (MI6). Whereas the RSS was listening into German intelligence, the Y-Service (Y being short for Wireless Intercept) was listening into military traffic. The Y service had twenty four major intercept stations around the country with sixty direction finding stations. Y-Service intercepts were also sent to Bletchley Park. Megg House is based on one of these listening stations. Radio direction finding vans were also in use and some of the scenes in the book are based on their work.

Bletchley Park is often referred to as Station X but, in fact, Station X was a tiny radio station in the roof of the Bletchley Park mansion. It was set up in August 1939 purely for MI6 to use to contact their agents in neutral countries. Station X was later moved, in 1940, to

Whaddon Hall close to Bletchley Park. For the purpose of this book Station X is used to describe Bletchley Park in 1940.

The work of the RSS is little known today, as is the contribution of the Girl Guides. In her wonderful book *How The Girl Guides Won the War*, Janie Hampton writes that, in Britain, the Guides were called upon again and again to help raise funds for the War effort, support evacuees, take messages for the Home Guard, administer First Aid and even put out incendiary devices. And, yes, they learned Morse code. In fact, Hampton writes that Guides were able to take their telegraphist badge which required them to construct their own wireless receiver and send messages in Morse code at a speed of 30 letters per minute.

The work of the Guides however did not go completely unrecognised. Even the Prime Minister Winston Churchill took off his hat to salute the Guides as they marched past at the 1942 Lord Mayor's Show in London.

The town of Orethorpe is roughly based upon Grantham in Lincolnshire which, as a wartime industrial town producing munitions, was repeatedly bombed by the Germans. Warrington in Cheshire was another source of inspiration for the town as is Gainsborough, also in Lincolnshire, another town with a manufacturing past. The shopping centre on the site of the former Langleys factory (in the 2010 Orethorpe) is inspired by Marshalls Yard in Gainsborough which is a modern shopping area built on the site of Marshalls factory.

The terrible night of bombing in the closing Chapters is loosely based upon the attack on Coventry on November 14, 1940.

About the Author

Sharon Edwards has been a journalist for more than twenty years, first in local newspapers and currently for the BBC, specialising in politics and investigations. She has won several journalism awards.

She was born in Lincolnshire and has lived there all her life.

She has a passion for history, including local history and the Second World War. The Most Dangerous Spy was inspired by Lincolnshire's role in early military wireless listening, starting in the 1920s, and also the role of the RAF stations and personnel operating in Lincolnshire during the war itself.

Her hobbies are cooking, cycling - and writing!

For more details, plus background articles, go to:
www.sharon-edwards.co.uk

Lightning Source UK Ltd.
Milton Keynes UK
UKHW042104121122
412087UK00001B/103